THE WAYS OF PARADISE

Born in Stockholm in 1942, Peter Cornell is a writer, historian and art critic. He taught theory and history of modern art at the University of Arts, Crafts and Design (Konstfack) and the Royal Institute of the Arts (Kungliga Konsthögskolan) in Stockholm, and is an honourary member of the Royal Swedish Academy of Fine Arts (Konstakademien).

Saskia Vogel is the author of *Permission*, the translator of over twenty Swedish-language books and the deputy editor of *Erotic Review*. Her work has been awarded the Berlin Senate grant for non-German literature and the Bernard Shaw Prize. Born and raised in Los Angeles, she now lives in Berlin.

'In *The Ways of Paradise*, notes on a vanished text become clues into a mystery: if the world has a centre, what is located there? Traversing holy cities, land art and myths of eternal return, Peter Cornell leads us into a maze of profound depth, unlocked at last in Saskia Vogel's exquisite translation.'
— Anna Della Subin, author of *Accidental Gods*

'Like a collision between the fantastical libraries of Borges, David Markson's art obsessed micronarratives and Iain Sinclair's occult strain of psychogeography. *The Ways of Paradise* is a labyrinth I never wanted to escape.'
— Chris Power, author of *A Lonely Man*

'Open, allusive, constantly expanding its appreciation of the covert relations between culture and history, place and belief, *The Ways of Paradise* embodies its own utopian premise. No longer are fragments deployed only formally; rather they serve as waymarkers on a quest to the interior, the final labyrinth of human imagination, and the mind's own mysterious corridors. Each traveller will find their own entrance, and each will surely be entranced.'
— Gareth Evans

'*The Ways of Paradise* is a work of art, an end in itself, a rich and enigmatic book.'
— Kristoffer Leandoer, *Aftonbladet*

'A stimulating and incredibly elegant anti-essay.'
— Jan Söderqvist, *Svenska Dagbladet*

'The subjects are woven together in a way that is as intelligent as it is imaginative. Cornell's book is proof of the author's erudition ripened into wisdom. Cornell's labyrinth lives and will live as long as there are readers.'
— Crispin Ahström, *Göteborgs-Posten*

Fitzcarraldo Editions

THE WAYS OF PARADISE

NOTES FROM A
LOST MANUSCRIPT

PETER CORNELL

Translated by
SASKIA VOGEL

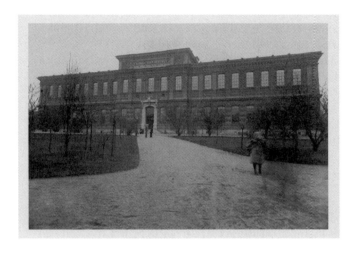

National Library of Sweden (Kungliga Biblioteket),
Humlegården Stockholm

Preface

The author of this text was a familiar figure at the National Library of Sweden in Stockholm's Humlegården. Almost every day for more than three decades he could be spotted in the serene reading room, absorbed in his studies, in reverie. It was said that he was occupied with an uncommonly comprehensive project, a work that – as he once disclosed in confidence – would reveal a chain of connections until then overlooked.

However, even after the thorough investigations following his death, the work in question has yet to be located. Among his effects is a sheaf of papers on which is written 'The Ways of Paradise: Notes', which is to say, all that seems to remain of his great work is its critical apparatus.

The found manuscript is typewritten on white A4 paper. It consists of 122 loose sheets, collected in said sheaf. Neither the pages nor the notes are numbered. In this edition I have, however, numbered the notes following their order in the manuscript. The extent to which this order was finalized we cannot be sure; other combinations cannot be ruled out. Nor can we be sure that this manuscript contains the complete critical apparatus to *The Ways of Paradise*, or if this represents but a small part. Certain graphic figures were included in the manuscript; other illustrations, notably reproductions of various artworks named in the text, I have appended myself.

As the author's sole remaining friend and student, all that is left for me to do is to publish these notes, in the hope that they will provide a glimpse of the lost work's contours.

Peter Cornell, Stockholm, June 1987

I.

1. Various types of fantastical tales, 'contes fantastiques autour des contes originaires'. Jurgis Baltrušaitis, *La quête d'Isis: Essai sur la légende d'un mythe*, 1985.

2. Ibid.

3. 'The centre of the world', 'the heart of the world'. This concept recurs in all cultures even as their geographic and topographical situations may vary: country, cave, mountain, tower, temple or city. These imagined places arise from fantasies of a holy land, described as follows by René Guénon: 'This "holy land", above all others, it is the finest of lands per the meaning of the Sanskrit word *Paradesha*, which among the Chaldeans took the form of *Pardes* and *Paradise* in the Western world; in other words it refers to the "earthly paradise" that constitutes the point of departure in each religious tradition.' Here was the origin, here was spoken the first, creative Word. See 'Les gardiens de la Terre sainte' (1929), in *Symboles fondamentaux de la Science sacrée*, 1962.

4. Possibly in André Breton's object *Souvenir du paradis terrestre* from 1953, a rugged rock, 11.5 x 9.5 x 5 cm, its title inscribed into the rock.

5. 'Paradise', from Old Persian *pairidaeza*, meaning 'enclosed garden, park'.

6. On parks as places 'where the city dwellers' wild dreams stir', see Louis Aragon, *Le paysan de Paris*, 1926.

7. Observe that he '*imagines himself* [sic!] to know'.

8. Cf. here Prof. Gianfranco Ravasi, for whom the term *centre* – 'paradise', 'cosmic navel' – is fundamental to descriptions of Jerusalem. The term can be read metaphorically, as a protective circle, a place of refuge, a *hortus conclusus*. *La Gerusalemme celeste*, 1983.

9. It was thought that mankind was created in the centre of the world, in the navel of the earth, *omphalos*. Mircea Eliade has recounted several such myths, among them Mesopotamian and Jewish. Of course, paradise, where Adam was created from dust, lay at the centre of the cosmos. And according to one Syrian tradition Adam was created in the very place where Jesus's cross was to be raised. The same notion has been preserved in Judaism, where Midrash, one of the oldest methods of biblical exegesis, identifies Jerusalem as the site of Adam's creation. Adam was buried in the very spot of his creation, at the centre of the world, on Golgotha. Cf. Mircea Eliade, *Le Mythe de l'éternel retour*, 1949.

10. Regarding Melchizedek as 'king of the world', ruler of Salem and the midpoint of the world, see René Guénon, *Le Roi du monde,* 1958, as well as Heb 7.

11. It can, by the way, be noted that within Jerusalem there are two places and – under the caliph Abd-al-Malik – three religions that could lay claim to the absolute centre of the world. On the one hand, there is the rock that provided the foundation for Solomon's Temple, the very crown of which marked the altar of burnt offerings; the same rock that was identified as the place of Mohammed's ascent to heaven. On the other hand, there is the hill Golgotha with the Holy Sepulchre, where the centre of the world is still marked with a bowl containing

a round rock. See Lars-Ivar Ringbom, *Graltempel und Paradies*, Royal Swedish Academy of Letters, History and Antiquities, 1951.

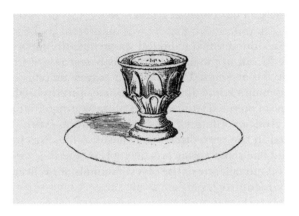

Omphalos in the Church of the Holy Sepulchre.
After Roscher.

12. The same rock is mentioned in Fredrika Bremer's travel notes from Palestine: 'Here they [the pilgrims] kiss a great round marble ball, which they called the "Navel Rock" and is understood to lie in the centre of the earth.' But the place – the Church of the Holy Sepulchre – otherwise instils in her noteworthy disappointment, 'a childish spectacle of a tasteless and false character. Devotion or edification thou wilt not perceive in it... My own celebration of Passover was above all interior.' *Lifvet i gamla verlden. Dagboksanteckningar under resor i söder- och österland* (Life in the Old World: Diary Entries from Travels in Southern and Eastern Lands), part III, 1861.

13. Referring here to the limestone Mount Tabor in Galilee, likely from 'tabbur', navel.

14. But can one not equally assert the inverse relationship here? Paul Cézanne's repetition of certain subjects doesn't have to mean that he was indifferent to the subject, that the motif was merely an artifice to render the desired form. On the contrary, his constant return to the mighty Mont Sainte-Victoire could suggest that this subject harbours a dark and mysterious meaning. Behind the outline of Sainte-Victoire we can perhaps glimpse old notions about the centre of the world. And via Cézanne this fantastical tale reproduces itself in ever-widening circles around its origin; this is how Peter Handke designates a specific geological point on this very mountain as his own centre point:

> In my quest for unity I had discovered yet another clue, to which I felt committed, though I had no idea where, if anywhere, it might lead. In the preceding months, every time I had looked at Cézanne's paintings of his mountain, I had come across this clue, and it had become an obsession with me.
> Seen from the west, where the mountain shows three prongs, it reveals its strata and folds in a geological cross-section. I had read that Cézanne as a young man was friends with a geologist by the name of Marion, who in later years accompanied him on many of his expeditions in search of "motifs". As I studied the maps and descriptions of the mountain, my thoughts began, involuntarily and inexplicably, to revolve around one and the same point: a fault between two strata of different kinds of rock. This occurs on the gently rising ridge path leading from the west to the actual crest, and it can fittingly be called a "point" because here, where one stratum penetrates most deeply into the

other, it also intersects the line of the ridge. This point, which in nature cannot be discerned with the naked eye, nevertheless recurs time and again in Cézanne's paintings, where it is indicated by a shadow line of varying length and thickness; even in the pencil sketches, the indentation is indicated by shading or at least by a delicate outline.

It was this spot more than anything else – I was about to start working – that impelled me to repeat the trip to Provence. From this new trip I expected the key; and even if my reason tried to talk me out of it, I knew that my imagination was right.

'Die Lehre der Sainte-Victoire', 1980 (The Lesson of Mont Sainte-Victoire, trans. Ralph Manheim, 1985).

15. Sainte-Victoire as seen from the quarry Bibémus. Dorival points out that in his autumnal years Cézanne developed a predilection for abandoned, desolate places, such as the forgotten, half-overgrown Bibémus. There he set up camp for a time, prior to having an atelier appointed on the outskirts of Aix-en-Provence a few years before his death. His landscapes from the Bibémus period, according to Dorival, all have 'un caractère cosmique de tragédie géologique'. Bernard Dorival, *Cézanne*, 1948.

16. In what follows, the discussion likely references the American sculptor Robert Smithson's work, made in extreme and inaccessible places, such as Utah's Great Salt Lake, Texan deserts or the Yucatán in Mexico – 'the unfocused fringe', in Smithson's own words. The aforementioned work *Broken Circle/Spiral Hill* (1971) was constructed in a former sand mine in the Netherlands.

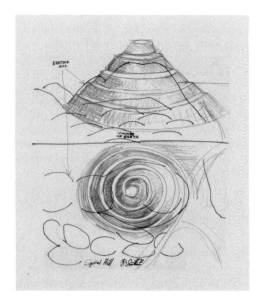

Robert Smithson, *Broken Circle/Spiral Hill* (1971)

17. It now seems to have been firmly established that Sigmund Freud climbed Vesuvius in 1902.

18. Cf. the French term *passages* in the art-historical literature about Cézanne (André Lhote, Erle Loran, etc.). Cézanne decidedly opposes the depth of field in the old one-point perspective – a static projection of the world in which imagined orthogonal lines converge at one vanishing point, or point of focus, in the distance. A one-point perspectivist representation presumes that the artist has viewed their motif from a single, arbitrary angle. The artist is in this case static, i.e. fettered to *one* point and unable to so much as turn his head, similar to the people in Plato's cave.

Aided by *passages*, Cézanne prevents the viewer from losing himself in the illusion of spatial depth and instead restores the background to the picture's surface. A person's shirtsleeve can, for example, take on the same colour as the drapery in the background, or a tree's contours can be split up and united with a mountain in the distance; this is how *passages* take shape, a constant transition between foreground and background, surface and depth. The eye of the beholder wanders as if at random, back and forth, across the image; they become a flâneur. Or, as Lhote expresses it, in Cézanne's landscape 'you can carry out an ideal walk, not on your feet, but with your mind'. André Lhote, *Traité du paysage*, 1939.

19. To whom he also appeals in the foreword.

20. The *passages* technique in painting develops right around the same time that the arcades (*Passagen* in German and *passages* in French) are being built in the great metropolises. They are later described as follows in *An Illustrated Guide to Paris* from 1852 (as cited in Walter Benjamin's *Das Passagen-Werk*, 1982): 'These arcades, a recent invention of industrial luxury, are glass-roofed, marble-panelled corridors extending through whole blocks of buildings, whose owners have joined together for such enterprises. Lining both sides of these corridors, which get their light from above, are the most elegant shops, so that the arcade is a city, a world in miniature, in which customers will find everything they need. During sudden rainshowers, the arcades form a place of refuge for the unprepared, to whom they offer a secure, if restricted, promenade – one from which the merchants also benefit.'

21. Clearly referring to what is in motion inside the arcades, the circulation of people, money and goods. In his novel *Le paysan de Paris* Aragon defines these spaces for trade, flânerie and unexpected encounters: 'How oddly this light suffuses the covered arcades which abound in Paris in the vicinity of the main boulevards and which are rather disturbingly named *passages*, as though no one had the right to linger for more than an instant in those sunless corridors.'

22. In Stéphane Mallarmé's full vision for *The Book*, which he planned but never saw through, radically new modes of reading are suggested. The reader was to abandon the rigidity of linear reading for 'a new way of reading, concurrent'. The reader could begin at the start or at the end of the work. And the pages, according to an intricate system, could be reordered so that new combinations and contexts of meaning would ever be arising. As such, *The Book* had neither a beginning nor an end, no fixed meaning, only perpetual circulation, like 'les anneaux mobiles du serpent', the snake's circuitous movements. See Jacques Scherer, *Le 'Livre' de Mallarmé*, 1957.

23. A paradoxical, cyclic motion it may seem: particulars are understood via the whole and the whole via particulars. As such, the very process of understanding, the hermeneutic work, in Heidegger, Gadamer, etc. can be described as walking in a circle, though not one that is closed, 'circulus vitiosus', but instead one that is freely circulating and ever-widening, moving towards broader horizons. Therefore, the expression 'hermeneutic spiral' is often preferred to 'hermeneutic circle'. Adrian Marino argues that 'the hermeneutic process is bound up with circular development. It runs through various circles,

which constantly convey a series of alternate connections, retreats, old paths with new credibility, a demonstration "in spiral fashion".' *L'herméneutique de Mircea Eliade*, 1981; see also Gerard Radnitzky, *Contemporary Schools of Metascience*, 1968.

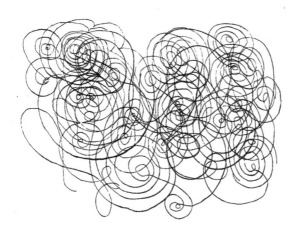

24. Their promenading and flânerie in Paris has no apparent destination and is guided instead by chance impressions. The Surrealists move as if automatically. Aragon writes in 1926: '[I] lived a chance existence, in pursuit of chance, which alone among the divinities had shown itself capable of retaining its authority.' Yet still not unconditionally, for the surrealists pointedly avoided all sites of note and picturesque tourist draws. They turn their backs on the Left Bank in favour of traversing a more ordinary Paris, like the Opéra quarter with its *grands magasins* and newspaper kiosks. But, in fact, this is highly volcanic ground, filled with sites that imbue the

passers-by with either euphoria or unease – street crossings, parks, statues, signs. André Breton calls for a map coloured by the surrealists' extreme sensitivity to *place*, where pleasant places are designated in white, repulsive places black and the rest grey. In this geography there are remarkable magnetic nodes such as the Tour Saint-Jacques, Place Dauphine, Parc des Buttes-Chaumont, the Opéra arcades. Cf. Marie-Claire Bancquart, *Paris des surréalistes*, 1972.

25. Ibid.

26. Here it is falsely presumed that a centre is always situated in a fixed location. Among nomadic peoples the situation differs, of course. Eliade offers one such example of a moveable *axis mundi*: the sacred pole of the Achilpa people of Australia. These people carry the pole with them on their travels. Proximity to the pole means that one is always at home, and through the pole a connection to the sky is opened up. Were the pole to break, however, it would be tantamount to catastrophe, bringing the 'end of the world' and a return to chaos.

The anthropologists B. Spencer and F. J. Gillen have observed the outcomes of one such catastrophe: the tribe's members were seized by death anxiety, roved aimlessly and, in the end, sat on the ground to await death. (Mircea Eliade, *Le sacré et le profane*, 1965.) Among Jewish people, the tabernacle, which denoted the presence of God, *Shekhinah*, was in constant movement until it found a fixed location when Solomon had his temple built.

27. The border city Perpignan was the centre of the world, according to the artist Salvador Dalí, for there the metre, the measure of everything, was formulated. He

also discovered that the city's train station inexplicably resembled the only drawing Sigmund Freud left behind.

28. It hardly needs to be pointed out that a centre may just as well be located at the periphery, like a humble fragment. Marcel Proust asserted that Vermeer's *View of Delft* was the most beautiful of all paintings, and when the painting was exhibited at the Jeu de Paume in 1921, not even his infirmity could prevent him from seeing it again. A photograph from this visit has been preserved, taken the year before his death. Proust has just stepped out into the bright sunlight and is standing erect, as if gripped by a grand, solemn ceremony. What has he seen? Proust incorporated the episode into his novel *In Search of Lost Time*. There the aged and sickly author Bergotte takes great pains to make his way to an exhibition to see the same painting by Vermeer, which he also loves. But this time, the whole doesn't interest him as much as an apparently inconsiderable detail: a little patch of yellow wall. At once the patch illuminates Bergotte's consciousness, ecstatic and merciless. 'His giddiness increased; he fixed his eyes, like a child upon a yellow butterfly which it is trying to catch, upon the precious little patch of wall. "That is how I ought to have written," he said.' Bergotte realizes that his writings have become ever more desiccated and lifeless, and he would gladly trade them for this exquisitely painted yellow patch.

This scene may recall the moment when Roland Barthes, in *Camera Lucida*, focuses on and is overwhelmed by the photograph's 'punctum', the point that has the ability to puncture, to make a hole. Barthes doesn't reach this point by way of system-building, no – 'punctum' takes him by surprise only once he allows his eye to wander over the image without bias. The punctum might then reveal itself to be something as seemingly inconsequential as a pair of shoes at the edge of a group portrait.

29. This woodcut from the Middle Ages represents the earthly Jerusalem, an imperfect and transient copy of the heavenly Jerusalem that God created at the same time as paradise. In the centre we see Solomon's Temple surrounded by several defensive walls. The city takes the shape of a spiral or labyrinth – the very function of which is to protect its centre.

Cf. here Bernard Gorceix's note in the critical commentary to a seventeenth-century Rosicrucian manifesto: 'The alchemist loves to compare his work to a perilous journey towards a city surrounded by walls.' *La Bible des Rose-Croix*, 1970.

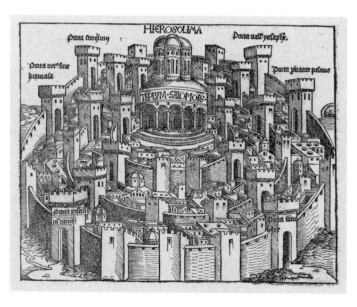

30. In the Bible the great cities are often compared to women: Babylon, Rome and Jerusalem. In both the Old and New Testaments Jerusalem is invoked as feminine, as a bride, virgin or mother; in the Apocalypse of St John, for example, it is said that the New Jerusalem is 'prepared as a bride adorned for her husband'. And Gianfranco Ravasi (*op. cit.*) has noted the many explicit analogies drawn between Jerusalem and a woman's, especially a pregnant woman's, womb. 'As we have seen the sacred space is a maternal womb, to which belongs an ideal *regressus ad uterum*; where one has been born, where one finds peace, security, nourishment, warmth, gentleness; where one lives as if in paradise.' Cf. here the medieval notion, still alive in a few of Leonardo da Vinci's anatomical drawings, of the womb shaped as a labyrinth or a spiral-shaped shell.

31. Beehive.

32. Leonardo da Vinci's and Dürer's labyrinthine 'knots' without beginning or end can be seen as maps of the universe. They are, along with a few late drawings, the kind of hieroglyphs that may have been stimulated by Leonardo's well-known exercises around the imaginative eye – to lose one's self in the damp patches on a wall or other fragmentary forms. 'One gets the impression that the [Leonardo] drawings held at Windsor Castle, which symbolically represent the world at once in its birth and its final cataclysm, stem from similar visions.' See Gustav René Hocke, *Die Welt als Labyrinth*, 1957; Ananda K. Coomaraswamy, 'The Iconography of Dürer's "Knots" and Leonardo's "Concatenation"', in *Art Quarterly*, 1944.

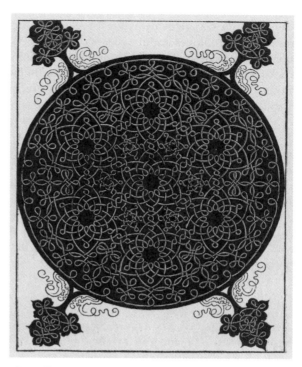

One of Dürer's 'knots'

33. 'The Infinite Labyrinth.' This is how Parker Tyler characterizes Jackson Pollock's large, abstract drip-paintings from around 1950. Traces of running and dripping paint create a rhythmic, elusive calligraphy as they layer, infinite like the cosmos or microcosmos. In this system of 'multiple labyrinths' layered on top of each other, a way out cannot be found and the central point has been camouflaged and annulled via multiplication. 'A mere unitary labyrinth, however, is simple, while in the world of Pollock's liquid threads, the colour of Ariadne's

threads affords no adequate clue, for usually threads of several other colours are mixed with it and the same colour crosses itself so often that alone it seems inextricable.' Like Leonardo's and Dürer's eternal knots, Pollock's paintings too lack a centre. Cf. Parker Tyler, 'Jackson Pollock: The Infinite Labyrinth', in *Magazine of Art*, 1950.

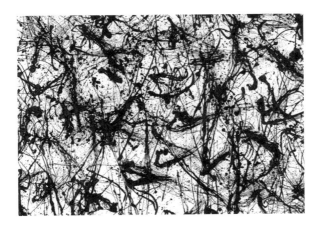

34. Bachelard refers to the old – the age-old – fantasies of men of science: their awe at the uncommon union between a hard, rough shell and an interior filled with soft, wet organic life. These dreamers have readily noted the analogy between the shell and a woman's womb or, among the more timorous, between shell and 'vagina dentata'. The shell is indeed present both in fertility and death rituals, a symbol of birth, into this life or into another. Such fantasies are a poetic form of knowledge and Bachelard has described them in *La poétique de la rêverie*, 1960: 'There are reveries so deep, reveries which help us

descend so deeply within ourselves that they rid us of our history. They liberate us from our name. These solitudes of today return us to the original solitudes. These original solitudes, the childhood solitudes leave indelible marks on certain souls. Their entire life is sensitized for poetic reverie, for a reverie which knows the price of solitude.'

This is, literally at least, regressive dreaming, seeking one's retreat in the shell, where one can close one's self in and bide one's time sheltered. In its shell, the snail takes refuge in the deepest point of the spiral, all alone. Bernard Palissy, the French ceramicist from the sixteenth century, indulged in such fantasies himself. In his major work *Recepte véritable*, he conceives of a 'fortress city' that could safeguard against all external peril. This town's construction is modelled on that of a shell, a murex specifically. From the central square where the governor resides the streets unfurl in spirals, of which the final one constitutes the city's outermost wall. See Gaston Bachelard, *La poétique de l'espace,* 1957.

35. The daydream as play transformed. Here he alludes to a passage by Freud in 'Creative Writers and Day-Dreaming' (1908): 'The creative writer does the same as the child at play. He creates a world of phantasy which he takes very seriously...instead of *playing*, he now *phantasizes*. He builds castles in the air and creates what are called *day-dreams*.'

36. To make a case against reverie, contrary to André Breton's appeal in the *First Manifesto of Surrealism* (1924) to consider 'the case against the realistic attitude'.

37. 'For she had alarmed me by saying to me of this church as of other buildings, of certain pictures: "What a pleasure

it would be to see that with you!" This pleasure was one that I did not feel myself capable of giving her. I felt it myself in front of beautiful things only if I was alone or pretended to be alone and did not speak.' Marcel Proust, *In Search of Lost Time. Sodom and Gomorrah.*

38. Bachelard nonetheless persists, apropos Jung-Stilling's *Das Heimweh*, in saying that 'the path in these so divergent forms of initiation is always that of a labyrinth'. And a little later, regarding the Freemason theme in George Sand's *La comtesse de Rudolstadt*: 'Every initiation is a test of solitude. There is no greater solitude than that of the labyrinth dream.' *La terre et les rêveries du repos*, 1948. Cf. Mircea Eliade, *L'Épreuve du labyrinthe*, 1978.

39. Here referring back to *Labyrinth of the World and Paradise of the Heart* by John Amos Comenius (Komenský) from 1631. Cf. the description of 'Mundus' (the world) in Cesare Ripa's *Iconologia*, the great iconographic lexicon from 1593, fundamental to allegorical representations in European art. In the German editions from the 1700s, a *fatto*, a fact or episode has been added in the background that underscores the allegorical content. In the background of Mundus we see a labyrinth as the symbol of life on Earth.

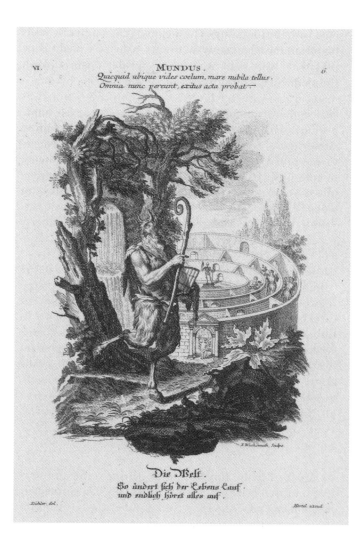

40. During the Roman Empire the labyrinth was associated with the founding of new cities. When new city walls had been raised, equestrian events – the so-called Game of Troy – were held in which each rider's path took on the shape of a labyrinth. Via this form the ride became a magical act through which the walls' impenetrability was sealed; therewith the city would become as unbreachable as Troy, which could, of course, only be conquered by subterfuge. Hermann Kern explicitly states that in the Game of Troy, 'die *Abwehrfunktion* [defence function, a warding off; italics mine] dieser Mauern auf magische Weise verstärkt werden'. This is why representations of walled cities are so often found in the Roman mosaic labyrinths along the Mediterranean and in more northerly parts of Europe. See Hermann Kern, *Labyrinthe*, 1982.

41. Jerusalem was one of the best fortified cities in the Middle Ages. Faced by its walls the crusaders despaired of ever being able to take the city. But then, it is said, the dead bishop Adhemar appeared and urged them to hold a three-day-long fast and walk barefoot around Jerusalem's walls; if they did so while in prayer and with repentant hearts, then they would conquer the city within nine days. On 8 July 1099 a solemn train of bishops, priests, knights, footmen and pilgrims circled the walls, barefoot all. Barely a week later the city fell to the crusaders' attack. Paul Alphandéry, *La Chrétienté et l'idée de croisade*, 1954; Steven Runciman, *A History of the Crusades*, 1951–54.

42. I consider the function of forgetting to be a protective and defensive manoeuvre, *Abwehr*. The protective mechanism of forgetting often takes on a labyrinthine structure. In *The Psychopathology of Everyday Life*, Sigmund Freud reconstructs a sudden gap in his memory.

He recounts an occasion on which he was unable to recall the name of the master who painted the grand frescoes of the Last Judgement in Orvieto; the name itself seemed to have inexplicably gone missing. 'Instead of the lost name – *Signorelli* – two other names of artists – *Botticelli* and *Boltraffio* – obtruded themselves, names which my judgement immediately and definitely rejected as being incorrect.' Freud's bewildering forgetting occurred during a train journey between Ragusa, Dalmatia and a station in Herzegovina. Freud had entered into conversation with a fellow traveller, and at one point Freud asked the man if he'd ever visited Orvieto and there seen the famous frescoes. Shortly before, they had been discussing the customs of Turkish people in Bosnia and Herzegovina, and in this context the sentence 'Sir (Herr), what can I say?' arose (even the most difficult news was imparted to patients with such stoicism, according to one of Freud's medical colleagues), as well as the place name Trafoi (where Freud had found out that a patient of his had committed suicide because of an incurable sexual disturbance).

These words had aroused certain unpleasant associations of death and sexuality in Freud, and he had tried to escape the unease by changing the subject: this is why he'd suddenly posed the question about the Orvieto frescoes. In his reconstruction of the conversation, Freud notes: 'I wanted to forget something, I *repressed* something. To be sure, I wished to forget something other than the name of the master of Orvieto.' And he analyses every swing and roundabout of forgetting and repression in a diagram that brings to mind a labyrinth's elaborate system of fortification.

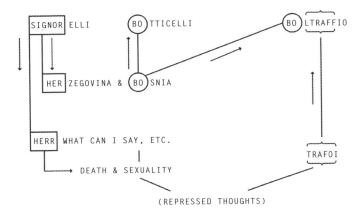

43. Can Hélène Smith's Indian journey be understood as an *Abwehrpsychose*, 'a defensive psychosis'? With this term Théodore Flournoy makes reference to an earlier work by Freud and Breuer on hysteria, when he in his own book, *Des Indes à la planète Mars* (1899), seeks possible explanations for the medium Hélène Smith's elaborate and visionary stories of her past life in fifteenth-century India. As he writes, '*Abwehr* has taken the form of a somnambulist novel.' Her remarkable fabulating could, then, have a defensive, diverting function that is meant to protect her from barely repressed volcanic impulses. Was she simply, as André Breton would later suggest, passionately in love with Flournoy, who conducted the experiment over the course of many séances in Geneva? By the way, in the library Freud left behind, the aforementioned book by Flournoy, a colleague from the infancy of psychoanalysis, was found.

29

44. The obviously absurd claim that he had been a courier of the secret atomic bomb, that he'd participated in the Spanish Civil War, etc. In a statement from October 1952 doctors Gunnar Inghe and Gustav Jonsson noted: 'In Enbom's group of symptoms, no matter how it is labelled in psychiatric terms, fabulation itself is an essential characteristic.' On Enbom as a daydreamer, see in particular Arne Trankell, *Chef för Grupp Norr: En dagdrömmares fantasier i skuggan av det kalla kriget* (Head of the North Group: A Daydreamer's Fantasies in the Shadow of the Cold War), 1974.

45. Among other reasons for discord.

46. For the devout Christians who were prevented from embarking on the arduous, perilous and costly pilgrimage to Jerusalem, an alternative was offered in the great cathedrals of northern France; a journey in miniature and in symbolic form. In Amiens, Arras, Chartres, Poitiers, Reims, Saint-Quentin and other places, a section of the nave's floor was taken up by a labyrinth, as an intarsia mosaic in dark blue and white marble. In Chartres it has a diameter of nearly 13m, and the length of the paths measure approximately 260m. In a roundabout way, here at the centre of the labyrinth one could reach Jerusalem. In place of the actual road to Jerusalem, the penitent, in prayer and singing hymns, would crawl on their knees along the labyrinth's paths and passages so as to finally reach the 'centre of the world'. As such, these church labyrinths were often called 'Le chemin de Jérusalem', the Jerusalem Way. Edmond Soyez, in his study *Les Labyrinthes d'églises* (1896), also mentions the name 'House of Daedalus' (in Chartres there used to be a copper plate of Theseus and the Minotaur in the middle of the labyrinth), while

Fulcanelli in *Le Mystére des cathédrales* (1925) references yet another term, 'Solomon's Labyrinth'. See also Paolo Santarcangeli, *Il libro dei labirinti*, 1967, as well as Hermann Kern, *op. cit.*

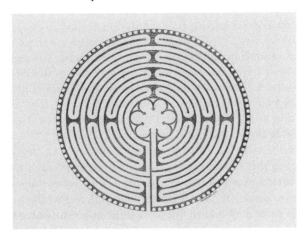

Plan of the Chartres labyrinth

47. 'He must have been struck by the similarity of certain religious ideas in pagan and Christian symbols,' Marcel Proust writes of John Ruskin in the preface to his translation of Ruskin's *The Bible of Amiens*. In a note on this observation, Proust makes specific reference to Ruskin's words on cathedral builders as the heirs to Daedalus: 'The first sculptor of imagery pathetic with human life and death' (i.e. the labyrinth).

48. An obvious anachronism. The term 'crusade' was not used during the Middle Ages; instead one spoke of the 'Jerusalem Way', the 'passage', or the 'pilgrimage'. Cf. Régine Pernoud, *Les Croisades*, 1960.

49. In medieval world maps one finds the Holy Land and Jerusalem at the very top. The East point of the compass, or the Orient, was located where later the North was placed. The medieval crusaders thus thought themselves to be travelling 'up' to Jerusalem. See Lars-Ivar Ringbom, *op. cit*.

50. Penance, of course, by choice or by force. The popes wrote letters of indulgence for the crusaders. To expiate sins and offences, being ordered to undertake a pilgrimage was not uncommon, for example Thierry, Count of Flanders, who beat an archbishop to death, or Henry II, after the murder of Thomas Becket. Other criminals might be instructed to walk in chains and leg irons to Santiago de Compostela. Here one might recall a most peculiar but overlooked story in C. J. L. Almqvist's *The Book of the Wild Rose*; it bears the name *Baron Julius K**. This wretched baron made a pilgrimage to Palestine. Before his astonished fellow travellers he said that he was travelling with no other goal but to 'fall ill'. After his death, Miss Eleonora finds in his library a black notebook with the inscription 'My Pilgrimage': 'I found stories not only and solely of the Holy Land, but also of events in Sweden: the people's – the poor, misguided people's – country.'

51. Ibid.

52. Here mention of the Children's Crusade of 1212 has regrettably been omitted – it should be said that it is very difficult to draw a clear line between the actual event and later myth-making. The Children's Crusade seems to have had its origin in the story of a twelve-year-old shepherd boy by the name of Étienne, who took up preaching outside the Basilica of Saint-Denis in Paris. He declared

that Christ had appeared to him and urged him to preach a new crusade. Étienne seems to have been in possession of a singular talent as a speaker, and he was believed when he offered assurance that the Mediterranean Sea would indeed part for the children just as the Red Sea had once parted for Moses.

A month or so later 30,000 children gathered at Place Vendôme; none was said to be older than twelve years of age. Enduring famine and serious privation, they made their way through France down to Marseille. Upon arrival in the city they rushed to the harbour in order to watch the parting of the sea. Though disappointed that the prophecy was not fulfilled, most stayed there, waiting, and a few days later they were offered free passage to Palestine. Seven ships were given at their disposal. Eighteen years then passed before they were heard of again, when a priest recently returned from the East recounted that two of the children's vessels had suffered shipwreck and sunk to the bottom of the sea off Sardinia; the other five had been boarded by Arabian pirates. The children had been taken to North Africa and sold as slaves, yes, a number of them had been sold in slave markets as far away as Baghdad. There eighteen children had been martyred upon refusing to convert to Islam. A small, lucky troop landed in Cairo, where they served as interpreters, translators and secretaries to the Egyptian ruler. See Steven Runciman, *op. cit.*; Paul Alphandéry, *op. cit*.

53. Concerning Mount Moriah, where Abraham was to sacrifice Isaac. On this mountain with the holy es-Sakhra rock, Solomon's Temple was built. It was rebuilt by Herod, and on the same site a mosque was constructed eventually. The master builder of Solomon's Temple is usually identified as one Hiram – not to be confused

with his namesake, the King of Tyre. Occasionally the name Adoniram is also put forth. The temple's elaborate measurements are described in detail in 1 Kings 6 and 2 Chronicles 3–4. For the floor of the inner sanctum a measurement of 20 x 20 cubits is given, and because the ceiling height is also 20 cubits, the room is a cube. The same measurements for the inner sanctum are again found in Ezekiel's vision of the temple (Ezekiel 40–43). The altar of burnt offerings in the forecourt outside the temple's eastern gate is also cubical. The altarpiece measures 12 x 12 cubits in Ezekiel's vision, 20 x 20 in Solomon's Temple and 28 x 28 cubits in Herod's version. The altar of burnt offerings constitutes the very crest of the holy rock. Odilo Wolff has presented a few diagrams of the temple's floor-plan that clarify the central placement and geometry of the altar of burnt offerings:

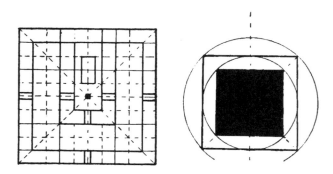

The altar of burnt offerings at the centre of the temple according to Ezekiel (left) and in detail (right). From Odilo Wolff, *Der Temple von Jerusalem. Eine kunsthistorische Studie über seine Masse und Proportionen*, 1913.

54. Written in a conceptual style, hard to read, moreover incomplete.

55. Mallarmé's calculations for *The Book*: 20 volumes of 384 pages each. 384 divided by 4 = 96; 96 divided by 4 = 24, the number of participants at each reading or 'séance'. The group of 24 is then divided into 3 = 8 people per group. Each place costs 500 francs. 8 multiplied by 500 = 4,000 francs, multiplied by 3 = 12,000 francs. Multiples of the number of pages seem to create a recurring variable: 384 divided by 4 = 96; 384 plus 96 = 480. Of *The Book*'s 20 volumes 24,000 copies are printed = 480,000 copies = 480,000 francs, etc.

The meticulous and involved calculations in Mallarmé's *The Book* recall the intricate measurements noted in Ezekiel's vision of the temple, with the altar of burnt offerings and the inner sanctum. Similar claims to perfection are also made, as in Jean-Pierre Richard's study *L'univers imaginaire de Mallarmé* (1961) which translates *The Book* to geometric architecture: 'When closed, *The Book* could be summarized as *cubic* perfection: height, length and width could be said to coincide and in this way create the figure of an exact formal adherence to itself.' This enclosed perfection causes Richard – using Mallarmé's own metaphor – to liken *The Book* to a gravestone, closed and yet open to eternity. But the loose pages create a dynamic counterforce, which, with the endless possibilities for reconfiguration, causes the stone to crack. Mallarmé writes in one of his drafts for *The Book*:

> cleanness light electr-
> – the volume, despite the im-
> pression of immobility, becomes, through this game, mo-
> bile – of death comes life

56. Here Scherer (*op. cit.*) suggests a parallelepiped.

57. Ibid.

58. Square and cube. In photographs of UNOVIS, the group founded by Malevich after the October Revolution at the Vitebsk Art School, we can see that his pupils have sewn a black square on their shirts as an emblem for a new age. A few years earlier Malevich had painted *Black Square*: the gateway to Suprematism. He called it the 'naked icon of our time ... a royal infant'. At the same time, he repeatedly praised the square's three-dimensional relative, the cube, with cryptic and bewildering pronouncements. The cube, he said, is 'a geometrical paradise, a symbol of the new eternity'.

Perhaps *Black Square* could be interpreted as the trace of a cube that has fallen flat onto a plane. In the fantastical speculations of yesteryear on the invisible fourth dimension, illustrations of falling cubes leaving traces on a two-dimensional plane often recur. With this meeting between two dimensions one can seek to make clear the analogue but barely perceptible encounter between a third and a fourth dimension – here the cube, until further notice, is made to play the role of the fourth dimension. In the slim classic by Edwin A. Abbott, *Flatland: A Romance in Many Dimensions* (1884), the novella's quadratic narrator, A. Square, ends up in prison because of his heretical speculations about a higher dimension beyond the two that already reign in his own flat Flatland. The conceit of the short novel's fictional preface is that A. Square is summarizing his fate for *Flatland*'s three-dimensional editor Edwin A. Abbott, an English schoolmaster with strong theological interests. What would happen in Abbott's own Spaceland if someone expatiated upon a fourth dimension? 'Would not you have him locked up? Well, that is my fate: and it is as natural for us Flatlanders to lock up a Square for preaching the Third Dimension, as it is for you Spacelanders to lock up a Cube for preaching the Fourth.' We are, like the flat beings on an even plane, incapable of understanding that the chaotic phenomenon of our existence, yes, even death itself, may but be a trace of a higher and more complete dimension. And when Malevich presented *Black Square* at the first Suprematist exhibition in 1915, there were several titles to be found that included the term *fourth dimension*.

Malevich's final and posthumous work was his own gravestone. It lies in the small village of Nemchinovka outside of Moscow, and is in the shape of a cube, painted with a black square. Malevich's pupil Suetin photographed it soon after the master's death in 1935, and the photograph itself seems to allude to Malevich's main theme: the relationship between a lower and higher dimension. Suetin photographed the gravestone straight on so that in the image it resembles and preserves the memory of suprematism's cornerstone, *Black Square*. And meanwhile we are aware that had he positioned himself only one step to the side, around the grave's corner, we would have beheld a higher dimension, a geometric paradise. Cf. Donald Karshan, 'Behind the Square: Malevich and the Cube', in *Kasimir Malewitsch zum 100 Geburtstag*, exh. cat., Galerie Gmurzynska, 1978; Robert C. Williams, *Artists in Revolution*, 1977.

59. Cf. the French critic Michel Seuphor's geometric artists' group Circle and Square, formed in 1929, with Mondrian, Vantongerloo and Torres-García as prominent members. With a strict use of geometry, they strove

for absolute purity and divine perfection. Several of them were clean-living men, vegetarians and absolutists. The Swedish author Gunnar Ekelöf had met such concretists in Paris and called them 'engineer Trappists'. After a visit to Mondrian's atelier Otto G. Carlsund recounts with amazement: 'I remember that there was a not a single speck of dust, all was clean. The walls, they were split into fields in the same manner as his paintings.'

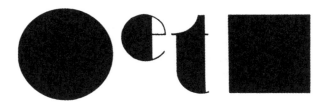

60. Square and cube. Here in reference to New Jerusalem in John's Book of Revelation 21:16–17: 'And the city lieth foursquare, and the length is as large as the breadth: and he measured the city with the reed, twelve thousand furlongs. The length and the breadth and the height of it are equal.' The New Jerusalem – cubic, mineral and crystalline – is imagined as an end-point in a cycle. The beginning, earthly paradise, on the other hand, is spherical, vegetative and organic. And the path from circle to square has been interpreted in an image of the circle's quadrature.

61. In Gérard de Nerval's *Voyage en Orient* (1851) the narrator's travel entries are constantly mingled with the romantic fruits of the author's reading. Immediate observations and impressions are interrupted by long fantastical tales that Nerval places in the mouths of various people the narrator happens to meet on his journey. A storyteller, connected to one of Constantinople's grand cafés, is given some 100 pages in which to tell the legend of King Solomon and Adoniram (or Hiram), the temple's indefatigable, genial yet misanthropic master builder. The temple building, one of the world's seven wonders, is described as a tremendous and fantastic enterprise for which more than 100,000 craftsmen had been put at Adoniram's disposal.

But three deceitful journeymen murder Adoniram because he refuses to reveal the master workmen's secret password. (The craftsmen are divided into classes, each with their own password: apprentices said 'Tubal-Cain', journeymen 'Shibboleth', and masters 'Giblim'). They then bury Adoniram's body and mark the spot with the bough of an acacia. The grave is eventually found by nine masters. They dig up the corpse and, faced with the rotted body, cry 'Makbenash', which means: 'The flesh leaves the bones.' This word becomes the masters' new password.

The story of the temple and the murder of Adoniram is a cornerstone in the mythologies and initiation rites of the Freemasons, and in *Voyage en Orient* it bears witness to Nerval's unquenchable interest in romantic, esoteric and fantastical stories woven around a legend of origin.

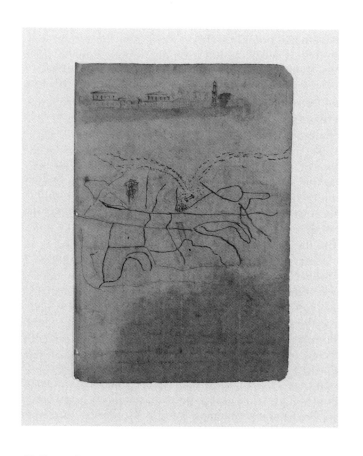

62. Lost, forgotten word. Hiram took this original, terrific password to the grave. 'Makbenash' then served as its substitute. The original word went missing, but authorities such as Jean-Pierre Bayard suggest that it is precisely the search for this 'lost Word' that is at the core of freemasonry. *La Franc-maçonnerie*, 1986.

63. On this point I can in no way follow the author's reasoning. It seems, to put it mildly, venturesome to use a 'novel' by Nerval as theological source material.

64. Nerval notes striking similarities between Druze and Freemason rituals and explains this connection via their common origin in the Knights Templar. In this sense, Druze ideas about Christianity are a memory from the time of the Knights Templar in the Middle East. The narrator in *Voyage en Orient* doesn't hesitate for a second over this breakneck genealogy: 'The Druze *akkal* is the Orient's Freemason. Freemasonry has, as you know, inherited the doctrines of the Knights Templar.' A Freemason himself, the narrator manages to avoid being expelled as an outsider and is granted audience with a Druze sheikh: 'I produced my title, having fortunately among my papers one of those handsome masonic diplomas full of cabalistic signs familiar to the Orientals. When the sheik again asked me for my black stone, I told him that the French Templars, who had been burned, were not able to hand their stones to the Freemasons, who had become their spiritual successors. It would be necessary to make sure of this fact, which is so far only a probability, but this stone must be the *bohomet* (little idol) which is referred to in the trial of the Templars.'

65. 'Makbenash.' Legend has it this word was cried out the night after Jacques de Molay, the leader of the Knights Templar, was burnt at the stake on Place Dauphine in Paris. Seven followers each took a handful of his ashes, threw it at the king's palace and exclaimed, 'Makbenash!'.

66. However, arrival can be experienced as a loss. Nerval writes to his friend Gautier: 'For a person who has never

seen the Orient, a lotus is still a lotus; for me it is only a kind of onion.'

67. Sources unanimously bear witness to the brutality of the crusaders. Often a crusade was launched as a Jewish pogrom in the homeland, in cities such as Mainz, Worms or Cologne; synagogues were burnt to the ground and several thousand Jewish people were murdered. Of the crusaders' gruesome progress during the invasion of Jerusalem in mid-July 1099, one eyewitness reports: 'Thereafter, upon the hour Our Lord Jesus Christ chose for our sins to suffer the torments of the cross, our knights, posted on the redoubt, fought with zeal, among them the Duke Godefroy and Count Eustache and his brother. At that very moment, one of our knights, by the name of Liétaud, stormed the city wall. Immediately the wall's defenders fled through the city and our band gave chase, cutting them down and slaughtering them until they reached Solomon's Temple, where they wrought a bloodbath so severe they waded ankle-deep in a lake of blood.'

Even those who were given sanctuary on the roof of 'Solomon's Temple' (then al-Aqsa mosque) by Tancred the Frank were killed without mercy. Thereupon followed indiscriminate pillaging. One eyewitness states that 'the whole city was full of dead bodies. The surviving Muslims were left to drag their dead beyond the city gates, placing them in piles that grew taller than the buildings. None before had heard of nor witnessed a bloodbath of such magnitude of a heathen people. Row upon row of pyres burned. Only God knows their number.' The massacre in Jerusalem shook the globe. The city was emptied of its Muslim and Jewish inhabitants. Many Arabs in the area had been prepared to accept the Franks as a force in the region, but with this all hope for coexistence was dashed. Far into the future this event would come to stand in the way of Christian-Muslim cooperation. See Paul Alphandéry, *op. cit.*; Friedrich Heer, *Kreuzzüge*, 1969; Régine Pernoud, *op. cit.*; and Steven Runciman, *op. cit.*

68. A conquest, a penetration with the character of a rape – the holy city as feminine, a bride or virgin.

69. 'Actually, Passaic centre was no centre – it was instead a typical abyss or an ordinary void.' Time and time again Robert Smithson sought out various places that instilled in him a certain dread and to which he gave the name *sites*. This wasn't about a taste for vantage points of great natural beauty or splendour – what André Lhote would dismiss as 'esthétique sportive' – but for abandoned, desolate and forgotten places, such as the Great Salt Lake in Utah, 'America's Dead Sea'; old industrial areas; quarries; desert landscapes or the dreary suburb of Passaic, New Jersey. His now-classic report from a visit to this unlikely spot was published in 1967 in *Artforum* magazine and titled 'The Monuments of Passaic'. With the seeming objectivity of an ethnographer and aided by a Kodak Instamatic, Smithson renders the city's overlooked monuments: an old bridge, a pumping derrick with a large pipe, a parking lot. Finally he stops in reverie in front of a sandbox, a 'model desert'. The whole text is given a certain charge – though it is never explicitly stated – by the fact that Passaic was Smithson's childhood home. On his journey back to childhood he finds a dreary and metaphysical place, in its endless tedium an iteration of eternity, of the entropy of aeons that is Smithson's paradoxical paradise: 'Has Passaic replaced Rome as the eternal city?' Since Smithson's death in 1973 – he died in an airplane crash

while photographing one of his earthworks from the air – many admirers have followed the artist's footsteps in pilgrimage to his ever more mythical sites.

70. 'Atterbom's lectures, known via the preserved manuscript in the National Library of Sweden, were not too preoccupied with their actual subject, an historical overview of the crusades. Palmblad, who was familiar with his friend's lovable habit of, as a rule, addressing something other than what he had promised, shared some of his misgivings with Hammarsköld on 21 March 1822. "He was meant", he notes, "to present on the crusades; he is, however, presenting on political science."' Carl Santesson, *Atterbomstudier* (Atterbom Studies), 1932.

71. Only a scant few have seen Smithson's *Spiral Jetty* in situ, so to speak, ruggedly located in the Great Salt Lake in Utah. When he saw it from the air Smithson compared its winding form to a gigantic 'drip painting' by Jackson Pollock. Today because the water levels have risen, the giant stone bridge or breakwater is less visible – it can only be faintly discerned as an underwater wall. Instead, we know the artwork from photographs, an essay containing Smithson's own documentation and the film he made around the development of *Spiral Jetty*. This material is said to create a *nonsite*, to use the artist's own terminology: a present-time documentation of an absent *site*, which is a kind of sign or symbol for the original place. Those who had the opportunity to see *Spiral Jetty* in the Great Salt Lake may have been disappointed, for the spiral structure only becomes apparent from the air due to its enormous scale. On site, the artwork was not in the first instance an object purely intended for spectatorship, but rather one to be moved through, literally gone through and passed

by, in that one could walk atop the approximately 500m long spiral towards the centre. 'He [Smithson] took giddy pleasure that the viewer coming to the end of the *Spiral Jetty* finds nothing there,' recalls John Coplans in 'Robert Smithson, the "Amarillo Ramp"', in Robert Hobbs, *Robert Smithson: Sculpture*, 1981.

72. 'Can one not affirm the nonreferral to the centre, rather than bemoan the absence of the centre? Why would one mourn for the centre? Is not the centre, the absence of play and difference, another name for death?' But on the other hand: 'Is not the desire for a centre, as a function of play itself, the indestructible itself? And in the repetition or return of play, how could the phantom of the centre not call to us?' Questions posed by Jacques Derrida in 'Ellipse', in *L'Écriture et la différence*, 1967.

73. Handwritten word illegible.

74. Hartman illustrates his reasoning with two alphabetic labyrinths by Jost Amman and Johann Caspar Hiltensperger, respectively. Hiltensperger's labyrinth unfurls from a few words taken from the apocryphal Book of Sirach: 'All wisdom is from the Lord...' The figure is logocentric; all meaning radiates from and can be traced back to the word at the centre. There is the origin, the truth and the guiding principle – the strict father who forbids deviation, pleasure-filled flânerie and improvised embroideries.

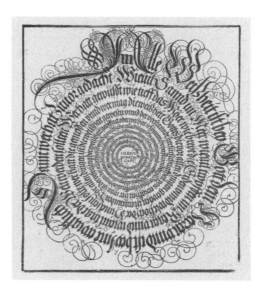

The first figure, by Amman, however lacks one such centre. Here, freely and organically, a series of *contes fantastiques* grow from a *conte originaire*, which is by now so overgrown that it may no longer be detectable. New meanings are spread, unexpected pathways open up, for the person who travels without a fixed route. 'It is a word cast on the waters, a prodigal without hope of return.' Geoffrey Hartman, *Saving the Text*, 1981.

The difference between the original text and the exegetic corresponds to the difference between the rabbi and the poet, according to Jacques Derrida in an essay about the poet Edmond Jabès. Allan Megill further interprets this reasoning in his book *Prophets of Extremity* (1985): '"Rabbinical" interpretation is the sort practised by Talmudic scholars, who keep a clear separation between

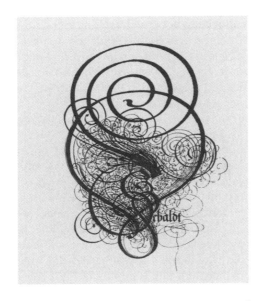

Scripture and Midrash, granting an unequivocal priority to the former and regarding the latter as a secondary working out and expansion of the Sacred Text. "Poetic" interpretation, the sort practised by Jabès, is a very different enterprise. Here the distinction between "original text" and "exegetical writing" is blurred if not eliminated, with interpretation itself serving as an "original text"... It [Interpretation] becomes an end in itself, no longer seeking justification in its attempt to reveal the meaning hidden in an "original text".'

75. In the travel notes.

76. 'Iterology' – Michel Butor's term for the science he, a touch in jest, founded or at least sketched out. Iterology has as its task an investigation of 'the journey' [*le voyage*]

47

and the connection between travelling and writing, reading and literary genres. To read and write, after all, implies, as a journey does, a type of transplantation: between words, by pen or eye, or through fantasies about other times and places. Often one reads during trips, and perhaps one writes then too, and the form of the trip itself can colour the text or vice versa. Butor sets in opposition two classical pilgrimages: on one hand Chateaubriand's *Itinéraire de Paris à Jérusalem* (1811), and on the other Nerval's *Voyage en Orient* (1851). These books offer examples of two differing modes of travel and ways of writing. Chateaubriand travels in a linear fashion and, so to speak, via the central perspective where the route runs resolutely to the majestic pilgrimage destinations of Rome, Athens and Jerusalem (though Butor could have added that on the way home Chateaubriand did indeed visit Egypt and Tunisia). His Catholic faith is absent of any fissure or doubt, and his self-assurance is as unabashed as his egocentricity. In Egypt he only manages to see the pyramids from a distance but still sends a man to carve his name into the Great Pyramid, next to Napoleon's. On his pilgrimage he sees what he expects to see, i.e. no big surprises. Not even the desolate emptiness in the Judean Desert can make him, even for a moment, abandon his steadfastness: 'When you travel in Judea, the heart is at first filled with profound disgust; but, when passing from solitude to solitude, boundless space opens before you, this disgust wears off by degrees, and you feel a secret awe, which, so far from depressing the soul, imparts life, and elevates the genius.' Chateaubriand travels with the aim of gathering material for an already planned novel about Christian martyrs, and he never once doubts that the truth awaits him in Rome, Athens and Jerusalem, pillars of the Western tradition.

Nerval, however, calls into question such a route and such a view of knowledge. Instead, he prefers to circulate among the places at the edge of that Eurocentric trinity and takes a long tour with Cairo, Beirut and Constantinople as its most important stops. He merely brushes past Palestine. Nerval's Orient is an indeterminate magnetic field without mid- or end-point. For him the centre has none of Chateaubriand's comforting self-evidence, but is both melancholic and elusive: 'In Africa people dream about India, as in Europe people dream about Africa.' Nerval's restless travels give his book a rhapsodic form, in which different levels of reality and genres unexpectedly mix. Because he seems to sense the emptiness of arrival in Chateaubriand's travel destinations and ways of travelling, he seeks out peripheries, fruits of his reading and hybrid forms to create an interweaving of Islam, Christianity, the Druze religion, esoteric myths and mundane impressions. Cf. Michel Butor, 'Le voyage et l'écriture', in *Romantisme*, 1972; Gérard de Nerval, *Voyage en Orient*, with an introduction by Michel Jeanneret, 1980.

77. A continuation was promised, but never materialized.

78. A utopian, total and ethereal book, 'into which the whole world flows'. Mallarmé seems to have already articulated this idea in 1866. In a letter from the same year (to Théodore Aubanel) there is an early hint: 'I have laid the foundations of a great work.' And a few weeks later we find out: 'I imagine it will take twenty years to write these five books that together shall constitute the Work.' Until his death in 1898 Mallarmé was preoccupied with the idea of *The Book*, and in the final years of his life he dedicated his mornings to working on it. By and by, 20 volumes

were planned with a structure and form based on intricate algebraic calculations. The absolute, final version of *The Book* was never completed, of course. The drafts and fragments that have been preserved – despite Mallarmé's explicit urging that they be burnt after his death – have the characteristics of a concentrated, hieroglyphic sketch across 202 manuscript pages, and are extremely difficult to decipher. The pages are of varying formats and were written by hand, sometimes in ink, sometimes in pencil. The text seldom runs in a linear fashion; rather, words and numbers have been grouped so that the pages resemble a sort of crypto-poetic diagram. Certain pages are blank, entirely without writing, and among them several pages have been folded down the middle, serving as a kind of folder for other pages. The draft suggests various motifs – hunting, yachts, balls and fireworks – but which are above all devoted to *The Book*'s form and architecture. Moreover, the manuscript contains a series of instructions for the reception of the work, i.e. its modes and forms of reading. The author planned to present *The Book* himself during so-called séances, a set number of pages at a time, for a specially invited audience, divided into groups of either 24 or 8 people. Because the loose sheets could be rearranged and each page thereto opened itself up to ten different types of interpretation, *The Book* held space to be rearranged in a great number of ways. Its entire structure resists the reader's attempt to find an unambiguous and fixed meaning; instead it is in constant metamorphoses. Yes, somewhere in the manuscript Mallarmé states there are interpretational possibilities of no fewer than 3,628,800 (a number that moreover appears in the alchemist Athanasius Kircher's *Ars Magna Sciendi sive Combinatoria* from 1699). The number of combinations is based on a strict calculation in which nothing has been left to chance – and yet chance seems to enter through the back door, for who can predict or keep themselves from being surprised by 3,628,800 combinations? As always with Mallarmé, *The Book* holds the tension between coincidence and calculation.

The Book could never be realized in physical form. Nonetheless the author's other works all seem to circle around this absent centre. As Jacques Scherer, who edited and published the manuscript in 1957, wrote: 'The greatness of Mallarmé's work stems from the total Book towards which it is oriented. The highlights in his published works bathe in a remarkable light, the invisible origin of which is the final and incomplete *The Book*.' Jacques Scherer, *op. cit*.; cf. Gustav René Hocke, *Manierismus in der Literatur*, 1959.

79. No, not in this context. Jacques Derrida's words refer to a work by Edmond Jabès, *Le Livre de l'absent*: 'Unwittingly, writing simultaneously designs and discovers an invisible labyrinth in the desert, a city in the sand.'

80. It is in *The Non-Objective World* (1927) that Malevich proclaims: 'No more "likenesses of reality", no idealistic images – nothing but a desert!'

81. More specifically, André Masson's sand paintings from the late 1920s. Masson would spread his canvas out on the ground, pour and squirt glue across it, then spread sand on top, all very quickly and without preparatory work. Jackson Pollock saw his work in New York – Masson had been given asylum there during World War II – and was greatly influenced by Masson's ideas and automatic technique. But when describing his own working process Pollock hints at another source. With the canvas on the

floor, he says, he felt nearer, more a part of the painting, since this way he could walk around it, work from all four sides, literally be in the painting. This is akin to the method of the Navajo sand-painters of the south-west. Because he spent his childhood in Arizona, Pollock was familiar with the Indigenous ritual sand-paintings made in the Arizona desert, southern Utah and New Mexico. These paintings often took the shape of spirals or labyrinths, as in those by the Navajo, which were composed in order to heal or cure, or as a fertility ritual. Dance was an important part of the ritual. The sand-painting's structure was worn away by the dancing and in the evening, after the ritual, its patterning had been scattered and erased.

Pollock's paintings, too, resemble the traces of a dancer whose movements are forever seeking to break down, balance and counteract the fixed and static structure that threatens to take shape. Rivulets of colour are poured on layer by layer and in this way his 'multiple labyrinths' arise. In the end a large macrocosmic or microcosmic flow of energy stands out in bold relief, in which everything is at once harmonious and in constant motion. Pollock's automatic, non-objective and spontaneous form has a clear parallel in jazz, all the more so in the contemporary bebop. A music that Norman Mailer, in his 1957 essay 'The White Negro', saw as the most important precursor of the hipster – the more physical and violent American variant of the European existentialist. The hipster, like the Black American, has created a secret and subtle outsider language. The rapid, fluid intonation gives language an abstract multiplicity that shields against an environment full of danger and threat. It is a language that can communicate all but that which is static. Mailer's characterization of the hipster's language could also be applied to the action painter Pollock's visual language: 'It is a pictorial language, but pictorial like non-objective art, imbued with the dialectic of small but intense change, a language for the microcosm, in this case, man, for it takes the immediate experiences of any passing man and magnifies the dynamic of his movements, not specifically but abstractly so that he is seen more as a vector in a network of forces than as a static character in a crystallized field.'

82. Namely, the traces of the dance. Kerényi seeks the origins of the labyrinth in the rounds of the circle dance (*Labyrinth-Studien*, 1950). Plutarch (ca. 50–120 A.D.) also connects the labyrinth with dance but inverts Kerényi's causal context. In his biography of Theseus he describes it accordingly: 'On his voyage from Crete, Theseus put in at Delos. Here he made a sacrifice to Apollo and danced with the youths a circle dance, a *geranos* or "crane dance" which they say is still performed by the Delians; a chain dance that in its rhythmic involutions and evolutions imitated the paths and whorls of the labyrinth.' Cf. the Scandinavian term *jungfrudans* or 'maiden's dance'.

83. There the author criticizes the slow pace of excavation, the lukewarm interest in the whole archaeological enterprise: 'Already in 1669, at an excavation site near Vesuvius, there had been found a few antique inscriptions, which make reference to a city by name of Pompeii; but one did not deem these reason enough to believe that it would have been situated in this region.' B.v. Beskow, 'Ett besök i Pompeii' ('A Visit to Pompeii'), *Svea* 13, no. 2, 1831.

84. Askelöf's papers, I.

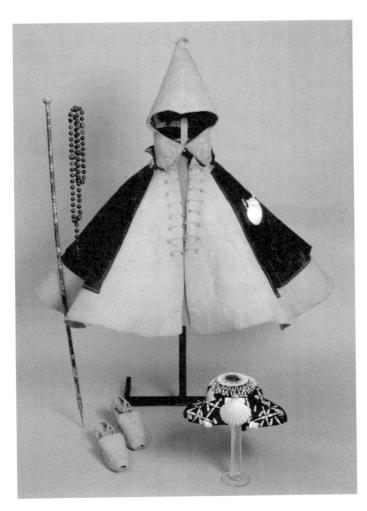

Pilgrim clothes belonging to Stephan Praun (1571)

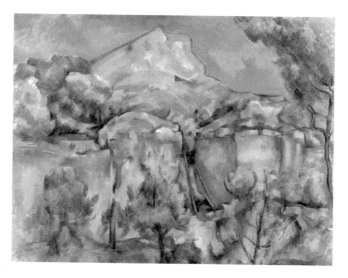

Paul Cézanne, *La Montagne Sainte-Victoire, vue de Bibémus* (1895–99)

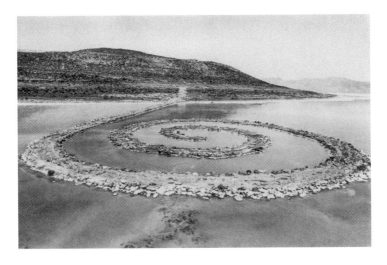

Robert Smithson, *Spiral Jetty* 1970

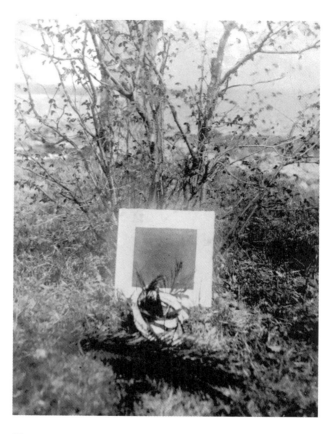

Photograph of the tomb of Kazimir Malevich, attributed to Nikolai Suetin (1935)

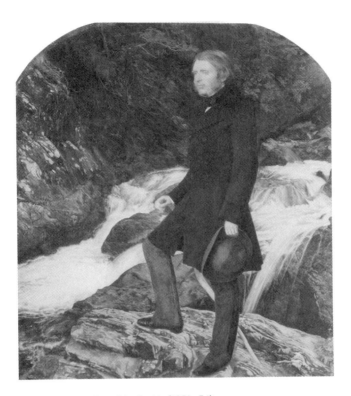

John Everett Millais, *John Ruskin* (1853–54)

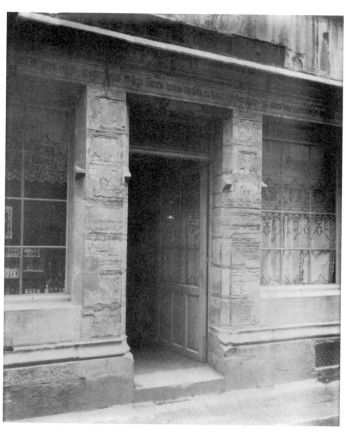

Eugène Atget, *House Known as Nicolas Flamel's* (c. 1900)

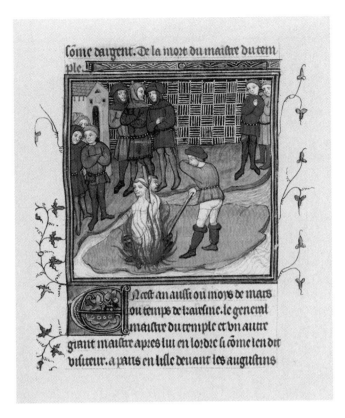

The Virgil Master, miniature taken from the *Chroniques de France ou de Saint-Denis* (c. 1380)

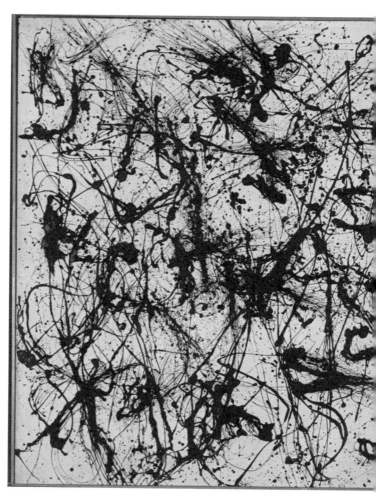

Jackson Pollock, *Number 32* (1950)

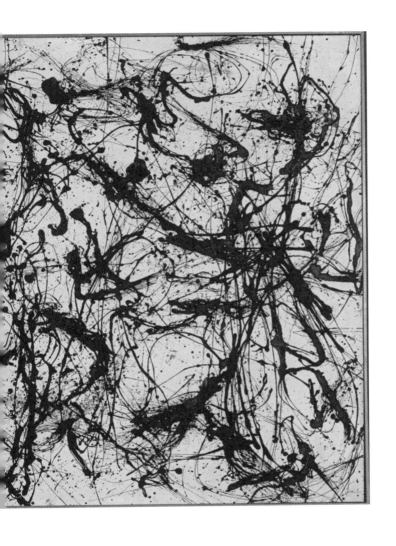

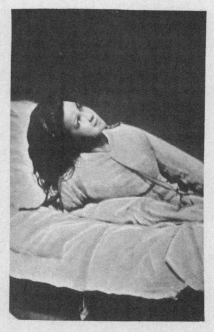

Photographs of Doctor Charcot's patients,
taken at the Salpêtrière (1878)

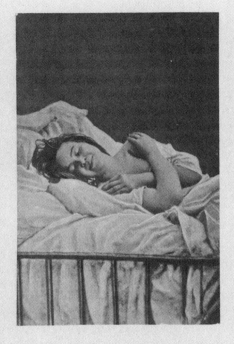

Planche XXI.

ATTITUDES PASSIONNELLES

EROTISME

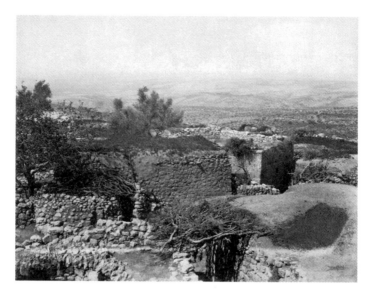

View of the Judean desert, Francis Bedford (1862)

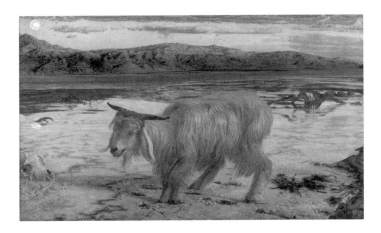

William Holman Hunt, *The Scapegoat* (1855)

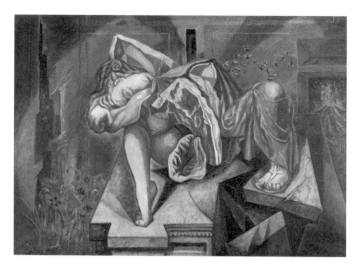

André Masson, *Gradiva* (1939)

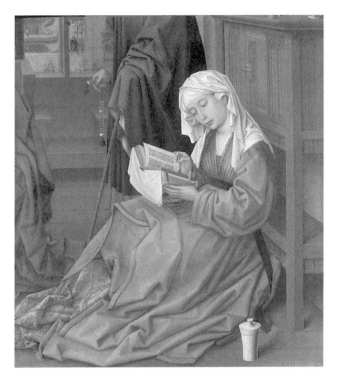

Rogier van der Weyden, *The Magdalen Reading* (c. 1435)

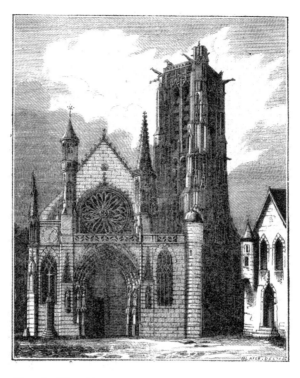

Church of Saint-Jacques-de-la-Boucherie

II.

1. In Paris, ahead of their departure to Santiago de Compostela, pilgrims would gather at the Gothic church of Saint-Jacques-de-la-Boucherie, the tower of which, Tour Saint-Jacques, still stands at rue de Rivoli between Châtelet and Hôtel de Ville. From here the same pilgrimage was undertaken by the legendary alchemist Nicolas Flamel (ca. 1330–1417), a poor writer who lived right by the church. One day by coincidence Flamel came across a remarkable old folio, which turns out to have been authored by the Jewish cabbalist Abraham Juif. The book contained alchemical texts and illustrations that Flamel and his wife Perenelle, despite their great efforts, could not decipher. But on the journey home from Santiago de Compostela Flamel happens to meet an old, learned man who helps explain the enigmatic pictures. This Master Canches, a Christian of Jewish origin, dies soon thereafter. Aided by his instructions, Perenelle and Flamel – by his own account in the apocryphal *Livre des figures hiéroglyphiques* – succeed in manufacturing both silver and gold. Be that as it may, Flamel, according to legend, became unexpectedly rich and the owner of a great number of properties, donated money to charity and to the restoration and ornamentation of churches, the enigmatic iconography of which was inspired by the images in Abraham Juif's folio. Flamel was buried in Saint-Jacques which – with the exception of the tower – was destroyed during the Revolution. Today Flamel's gravestone is preserved at the Musée de Cluny. His name recurs in surrealist literature, for example in the *Second Manifesto of Surrealism* (1929), in which Flamel's visual world is compared with surrealist painting.

2. The surrealist artist Jacques Halpern did not live far from the Tour Saint-Jacques on rue de Rivoli. He passed by it often, never paying it much notice – habit does have the power to render our everyday surroundings invisible. But one day the tower emerged before his eyes with unexpected clarity, and as he walked away from it, he heard himself mumble: 'La Tour Saint-Jacques.' Right then, a bus passed by, number 21, and at the same moment the clocks in the Palais de Justice struck three.

On the 21st of the same month, at 3 in the afternoon, using surrealist logic, he seeks out the tower. A stranger approaches him and they enter into conversation. The stranger relays that he has come to this place, apparently driven by an irresistible force – he who never otherwise leaves his apartment at 38 rue Saint-X. The two men part ways at the metro. Later Halpern seeks the stranger out at his address, but there too the stranger is unknown, and Halpern never lays eyes on him again.

André Breton recounts this episode in the afterword to *Arcanum 17*, the reason being that he himself on 27 April 1947 had set a date to meet his friends Jacques Hérold and Victor Brauner at the Tour Saint-Jacques.

3. This also applies to the modern metropolis. For example, Walter Benjamin writes: 'The city is the realization of that ancient dream of humanity, the labyrinth. It is this reality to which the flâneur, without knowing it, devotes himself.' *Das Passagen-Werk*, 1982.

4. By this description one should be able to draw the conclusion that the city's centre crystallizes in the areas around Pont-Neuf. Near the bridge abutment on the right bank, where the rue de l'Arbre-Sec spills out onto the quay, is – according to André Breton – the best view

of the Seine; from there it stretches out pleasingly like a mermaid in repose. On the other side of the bridge is Place Dauphine, which Breton visits on one of his rambles with Nadja and which imbues him with a very peculiar feeling: 'Place Dauphine is certainly one of the most profoundly secluded places I know of, one of the worst wastelands in Paris. Whenever I happen to be there, I feel the desire to go somewhere else gradually ebbing out of me, I have to struggle against myself to get free from a gentle, over-insistent, and, finally, crushing embrace.'

Twenty-five years later, in *La Clé des champs*, the author tries to clarify the composite feeling that the place evokes, scrutinizing it from a distance, with a kind of bird's eye view. The Île de la Cité is often said to be shaped like a heart, but rather it strikes Breton as having the shape of a woman. At the top towards Île Saint-Louis he sees her raised elbow, behind which she is shyly hiding her face; in the rest of the island he sees her torso. Now everything becomes clear: 'I find it unbelievable today that others before me, upon entering the Place Dauphine from the Pont-Neuf, were not grabbed by the throat at the sight of its triangular conformation, a slightly curvilinear one at that, and of the slit that bisects it into two wooded areas. Unmistakably, what lies revealed in the shade of these groves is the *sexe* of Paris.' Its forest, he notes, still burns, each year, in memory of the execution of the Knights Templar that was carried out on that spot on 13 March 1313. (Here André Breton mistakes the relevant point in time; the correct date is 19 March 1314. On this day the Templars' leaders Jacques de Molay and Geoffroi de Charny were burnt at the stake by direct order of King Philip the Fair, who was seized by rage after both of the accused unexpectedly rescinded confessions they'd previously made under torture.) The base of this triangular square borders the Palais de Justice. The sex's proximity to this seat of punishment explains to Breton the eerie atmosphere of taboo and pressure that the place emits. All this marks Place Dauphine out as Paris's sacred place, 'le lieu sacré'. Breton, *Nadja*, 1928. Cf. Marie-Claire Bancquart, *Paris des surréalistes*, 1972, and Mirella Bandini, *La vertigine del moderno*, 1985.

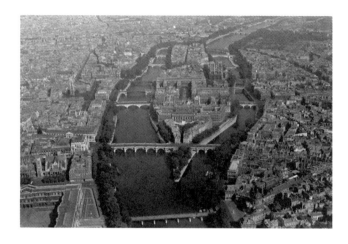

5. According to André Breton, who took the information from Fulcanelli, the rue de l'Arbre-Sec near to Pont-Neuf was named after an inn that in the 1300s housed pilgrims on their way to the Holy Land. The sign bearing the symbol of a dry tree – a biblical and alchemical symbol – remained in place until the 1600s. Breton, *op. cit*.

6. Pilgrims wore a rough tunic-like jacket, a small leather sack around the waist containing only the barest of essentials and carried a wooden walking stick. Around

these attributes a comprehensive symbolism developed: the walking stick was meant to help the pilgrim hold at bay wolves and angry dogs, that is to say the devil, and as a third leg it also served as a reminder of the Holy Trinity. On his jacket he might, upon return from the place of pilgrimage, affix a badge, a palm frond if he had been in Jerusalem. But another badge would eventually become more common. Yrjö Hirn recalls encountering it in a display at the Germanisches Nationalmuseum in Nuremberg: 'The jacket's collar is adorned with shells and upon the left breast a large shell has been sewn fast. The hat, its brim folded up at the front, is also richly decorated with shells, of which the largest, a scallop, is fixed in the middle above the forehead, whereas smaller molluscs, long, spiralled and narrow, are arranged in cruciform around the brim. An inscription states that this costume belonged to Stephan Praun from Nuremberg and was worn by him on his pilgrimage to the Holy Land in the year 1571.' Yrjö Hirn, *Eremiter och pilgrimer* (Hermits and Pilgrims), 1924.

Why shells, exactly (the kind that have given us the term *pilgrimsmusslor*, or 'pilgrim shells')? Hirn suggests that these souvenir scallop shells and molluscs, sometimes cast in tin or lead, originated with the pilgrimages to Mont-Saint-Michel in Normandy, which became one of Christianity's earliest and most distinguished destinations after it was said that the Archangel Michael appeared there in the year 708. 'The learned archaeologist Paul Gout has, in his great work on Mont-Saint-Michel, asserted that the pilgrims who visited this sacred edifice, after being forbidden by the priests to take with them pieces of the church wall or altar covering as souvenirs, began instead to remove small rocks or shells, of the kind collected from the seashore. These latter objects – with all the requisite marine associations – served best of all as displayed memories from the sacred place, in which the ignorant inland-travellers imagined seeing a final outpost of the mainland in the sea, a place "where one might not yet be in heaven, but one has already left Earth". It was a source of pride, in one's pious wanderings, to have gone the long way to the ocean, and so it became common custom to hang shells on one's costume upon leaving Saint-Michel.' Hirn, *op. cit.*

A similar legend is told of Santiago de Compostela (whence, via a series of wonders, St. James' remains had been relocated – the Holy Virgin's dwelling, via a miracle, is also said to have been moved from Nazareth to Loreto, Italy, which turned the place into a popular destination for pilgrims). It was said that a strange fish with a shell on each of its sides swam in the ocean beyond Santiago de Compostela, and it was these shells that the pilgrims collected and sewed to their clothing.

Shells and casts of shells soon came to provide a small souvenir industry, and they were sold at markets next to the cathedral in Santiago, in Jerusalem and in other sites of pilgrimage. Cf. Jonathan Sumption, *Pilgrimage: An Image of Mediaeval Religion*, 1975.

7. Here it could be interjected that certain cosmological dreamers, such as Ghyka, Hambidge, etc. believe themselves to have glimpsed the innermost order of the world in a spiral-shaped shell, the so-called nautilus shell. The spiral of this shell takes its shape according to a ratio of numbers in the same harmonious proportion to the golden ratio, which the Renaissance mathematician Luca Pacioli named the 'divine proportion'. The nautilus's spiral expands logarithmically based on the numerical series, 1, 1, 2, 3, 5, 8, 13, 21, 34, 55, 89, 144, etc. in which

each number is equal to the sum of the two previous. The ratio between the lower number and the higher one that follows makes the 'golden number', 1.618 (or inverted, 0.618). This number is said to be embedded in Creation, an example being the logarithmic spiral of the nautilus, but also the sunflower's corolla, nebulas of the macrocosmos and galaxies. And in humans the golden ratio meets the centre point that once connected us to our origins, the navel; at least, Ghyka asserts, this applies to the ideal human of the Venus de Milo type (readers, by the way, can use a tape measure to check if they are of a similar type: the golden ratio is obtained by dividing one's body height by 1.618 or multiplying it by 0.618). See Matila Ghyka, *Le nombre d'or*, 1931.

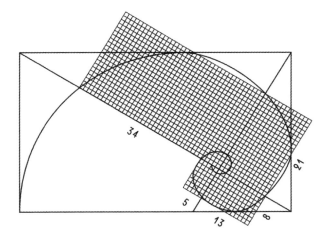

8. *Ibid.*

9. Already then a professor.

10. Alluding to the shell as a souvenir – cf. the madeleine in Marcel Proust's *In Search of Lost Time*. It is the taste of this cake, dipped in lime blossom tea, which in the famous scene suddenly awakens childhood memories from Combray, resurrecting the past. Proust describes the madeleine's shape: 'short, plump little cakes called "petites madeleines", which look as though they had been moulded in the fluted scallop of a pilgrim's shell.'

Isn't the narrator's memory a kind of pilgrimage to the lost paradise of the past? These, after all, are recollections that fill him with a 'precious essence'.

Actual pilgrimages can be found in Proust's biography too. Soon after John Ruskin's death in the year 1900 Proust wrote an article in *Le Figaro* titled 'Pèlerinages ruskiniens en France', where he encourages pilgrimages to the places Ruskin described, to the great Gothic northern French cathedrals in Amiens, Beauvais, Rouen. Proust, who would later take himself all the way to Venice in order to experience Ruskin incarnate in the city's stone, followed his own urging and set off with a few friends for Rouen. In *The Seven Lamps of Architecture* Ruskin's attention is drawn to the detail of a fold: carved into one of Rouen's cathedral doors is a modest but highly bizarre bas-relief figure resting his head heavily in his hands, 'vexed and puzzled in his malice; and his hand is pressed hard on his cheek bone, and the flesh of the cheek is *wrinkled* under the eye by the pressure'. As so often in Ruskin, and in Proust, the detail stands out as central. In his book *Marcel Proust* (1958), Richard H. Barker also makes note of this crease: 'While he [Proust] was still busy with these tasks and while, as it happened, he was re-reading the passage in *The Seven Lamps of Architecture* in which, to condemn modern machinery and extol medieval handicraft, Ruskin describes some figures in bas-relief on the north door of Rouen Cathedral, the newspapers reported Ruskin's death, and Proust immediately decided that he must make a memorial pilgrimage, obviously to Rouen. He must see the bas-relief for himself. He went with his friends the Yeatmans, approached the north door, and eagerly scanned the hundreds of figures, looking for the ones immortalized by the master. Finally Madame Yeatman said that she had found them, and there indeed they were – the dragons and the odd little man resting his head on his hand so firmly that his cheek was puffed out under the eye. Few figures on the door can have been more completely insignificant; yet Proust was quite satisfied.'

11. 20 Jan. 1900.

12. He says that the book is assembled of creases and folds, that it is born of the folded sheet, sometimes sealed, as in the stapled pamphlet. Its closedness is both religious and erotic. Mallarmé describes thus in *Chronique* the intimate rite of driving an ivory paper knife into the darkness between two as yet unslit pages. A newspaper's shamelessly full pages, however, dispel the mystery. And he continues in the prose piece 'Le livre, instrument spirituel', in *Divagations*, observing the pile of pages stacked upon each other: 'With regard to the large printed sheet, the folding is a sign, almost religious, which is not so striking as its settling, in density, presenting the *miniature tomb, indeed, of the soul.*' The very image of the fold, of that which is folded, is, Jacques Scherer says, one of Mallarmé's central motifs. Scherer, *op. cit.*

13. Very likely gneiss. Ruskin harboured a passionate interest in geology, and the location of J. E. Millais's

famous portrait is not happenstance. It was during a trip to Scotland in the summer of 1853 that Ruskin, his wife Effie and Millais found the gneiss rock in front of the waterfall. In the rock upon which Ruskin stands, grooves and folds run like waves, like a petrified analogy to the whirling waterfall and river, along with the water flowing in the background. This choice of scenography is surely a reference to Ruskin's observations in *Modern Painters*, where he describes the arrested movement of the gneiss as a form of frozen time, a memory of the mountain's volcanic, fluid infancy: 'The tremor which fades from the soft lake and gliding river is sealed, to all eternity, upon the rock; and while things that pass visibly from birth to death may sometimes forget their feebleness, the mountains are made to possess a perpetual memorial of their infancy.'

14. In his public and infamous divorce case, Ruskin's secret was brought to light. A gynaecologist could verify that his marriage with Effie had been 'unconsummated', and she was therefore free to marry J. E. Millais, whom she had got to know during a trip to Scotland.

15. Norbert Hanold had 'forgotten' his childhood love Zoe Bertgang and replaced her with the bas-relief. Zoe had, so to speak, been masked by the art object; in it were traces of her characteristic graceful gait, which led to Hanold calling the relief 'Gradiva' (roughly, she who steps along brilliantly or splendidly). It turns out that it is Zoe herself, of flesh and blood, who eventually becomes his Ariadne and leads him out of the labyrinth's shelter of oblivion and repression.

It was C. G. Jung who first drew Freud's attention to Wilhelm Jensen's novel *Gradiva*. Freud read it with enthusiasm and then wrote a short essay titled 'Der Wahn und die Träume in W. Jensens "Gradiva"', published in 1907. One theme in the novel is dreams and repressed impulses, which were naturally of interest to the pioneers of psychoanalysis. Might Freud also have felt a kinship with the archaeologist Norbert Hanold, the hero of the book? The young Hanold had devoted his life to his branch of scholarship and seemed to live entirely for his research. But during a visit to the Vatican Museum he was inexplicably gripped by the bas-relief of the woman whose graceful steps can be glimpsed below the folds of her dress, and he bought a plaster cast, which he hung on the wall in his study (Freud and other analysts subsequently did the same). Some time thereafter he had an anxious dream in which he found himself in Pompeii during Vesuvius's violent eruption in 79 A.D. And there, in a square, he suddenly caught sight of the Gradiva of the relief, alive and embodied. He followed her and she took a seat on the marble steps of the Temple of Apollo, where slowly, as if by metamorphosis, she took on the colour of the marble before being covered in ash from Vesuvius, the flowing lava of which soon buried the whole city.

After this dream Hanold's usual peace of mind was disturbed. Unsettled and restless, he set off on a journey to Italy and eventually ended up in Pompeii itself. Miraculously enough, wide awake and in broad daylight he again catches sight of Gradiva! Yes, she is alive and real, for she answers to his address, and good Hanold is perplexed. But, with patience, Gradiva sets him on the right path. It turns out that she is in fact called Zoe Bertgang ('Zoe', life; and 'Bertgang', roughly, 'she with the elegant gait') and, incidentally, is the childhood sweetheart of the archaeologist to whom he once lived next door in Munich. Hanold had buried his passionate feelings for Zoe deep in his unconscious. He could not however prevent her from making herself known in the bas-relief, which gave rise in him such an intense and inexplicable attraction, and to which he gave the name Gradiva, a substitute for Zoe's name which seemed to have been lost to his memory.

The analogy between the archaeologist and the psychoanalyst is clear. Freud surely could see himself in Heinrich Schliemann, who, layer by layer, dug down through ancient Troy. And Freud writes in his essay: 'In his [Jensen's] last simile, however, – of the "childhood friend who had been dug out of the ruins" – the author has presented us with the key to the symbolism of which the hero's delusion made use in disguising his repressed memory. There is, in fact, no better analogy for repression, by which something in the mind is at once made inaccessible and preserved, than burial of the sort to which Pompeii fell victim and from which it could emerge once more through the work of spades.'

16. Ibid.

17. Doctor of Letters B. Risberg, however, has charitably reminded me that in Epistles 1, 10: 24, Horace made use of a similar image of nature's intractability.

18. Edmund Engelman's photographs of Berggasse 19 reveal Freud as a passionate, if not manic, collector of archaeological material. Half his desk, and every other unused table surface and shelf is filled to breaking point with antique statuettes. Freud himself willingly admitted that his lust as a collector was exceeded only by his nicotine craving.

19. Archaeologist but also detective. In cosy Victorian milieus at Berggasse 19 and 221b Baker Street, Sigmund Freud and Sherlock Holmes, respectively, receive those seeking help. They listen to stories both strange and detailed, behind which they eventually bring to light a no less fantastical, secret or latent context. Often the key is an insignificant fragment that passes the layman by and, aided by this fragment, they reconstruct an absent whole (just as the archaeologist reconstructs the shape of a jug from a small shard thereof). They move as if in circles, in ever-widening rounds: in the light of a hypothesis, they find and interpret individual fragments that together provide a corrected and expanded hypothesis of the whole, which helps them to then find new fragments and so on. For both, their sharp wit is unsurpassed and legendary. And when the case is finally solved, it is noted down in literary form as a case study – in turn becoming material for countless histories and myths. Do not the titles of Freud's stories, 'Rat Man', 'Wolf Man' (in which he expressly refers to Sherlock Holmes) and 'Little Hans' stoke the imagination as much as 'The Hound of Baskervilles', 'The Man with the Scar' and 'The Adventure of the Engineer's Thumb'? It is also a feature of the genre that the text is occasionally interrupted by a small diagram of the crime scene or another location central to the story. Cf. Steven Marcus, *Freud and the Culture of Psychoanalysis*, 1984; Carlo Ginzburg, 'Clues', in *Häften för kritiska studier* (Journal of Critical Studies), no. 3, 1983.

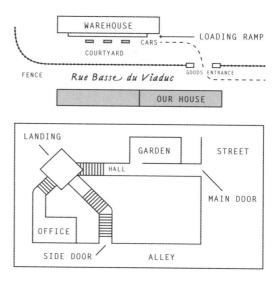

(haut) Freud, *Le Petit Hans* (bas) Conan Doyle, *Le Traité naval*

20. So too it has been assured, but when can the case be said to be solved and the excavations complete? Freud has described psychoanalysis as work not unlike the draining of the Zuiderzee. In place of the mysterious vegetation of the ocean's murky depths, what remains is a dry sea bed. It's a task that undeniably resembles that of Sisyphus, for don't new secrets arise throughout the working process and don't the work of dredging constantly create new furrows and leaks?

21. The Victorian era – during the latter half of the nineteenth century – sees the birth of the great metropolis and

therewith a new type of urban creature, the flâneur – a roving and curious observer of modern life. According to the encyclopaedia *Le Grand Dictionnaire universel du XIX siècle*, what marks out the flâneur is that he sees and hears what passes other people by; this could be apparently irrelevant phrases, fleeting sounds or innocuous situations. Here Walter Benjamin (*op. cit.*) makes an analogy with the detective: 'Preformed in the figure of the flâneur is that of the detective. The flâneur required a social legitimation of his habitus. It suited him very well to see his indolence presented as a plausible front, behind which, in reality, hides the riveted attention of an observer who will not let the unsuspecting malefactor out of his sight.'

22. 'Dodé né ci haudan té méche métiche Astané ké dé mé véche. 'In a trance, Hélène Smith repeats this phrase, which she has heard uttered on the planet Mars and which means, she elucidates: 'This is the house of the great man Astané, whom thou hast seen.' She takes somnambulant trips to Mars and reports on pastoral landscapes, lakes of blue and pink and peach-coloured earth. But further away, on Ultra-Mars, an indistinct planet beyond Mars, she seems to find herself at the outermost limit: 'I did not see any tree, any bit of verdure.' For several years in the late 1890s her speeches and writings and images were studied by Théodore Flournoy, the chair of the psychology laboratory in Geneva. The investigations took place during a great many séances during which the young, beautiful Hélène Smith automatically produced a number of astounding stories, languages, alphabets and images. Flournoy was an ardent opponent of spiritism and superstition and did not believe for a second that Hélène's words came from the spirit world; instead, he asserted, they were a rare fruit of her unbridled, childlike

fantasy world – her unconscious. But as soon as Flournoy tried to decipher her secret languages and visions, she would come up with new ones as a kind of defensive manoeuvre: after the Royal cycle – in which Hélène became Marie Antoinette incarnate – comes the Hindu cycle and then the Martian and, as a final outpost, Ultra-Mars.

Faced with the mystery of Hélène Smith, Théodore Flournoy and his assistants work like sharp-witted detectives to reveal her secret. When it comes to the Hindu cycle's alleged Sanskrit, Flournoy was aided by none other than Ferdinand de Saussure, the founder of structural linguistics. At this time, Saussure was working in Geneva as a professor of Sanskrit and Indo-European linguistics. He participated in a couple of Smith's séances himself. Cf. Sarane Alexandrian, *Le Surréalisme et le rêve*, 1974; Theodore Flournoy, *Des Indes à la planète Mars*, 1899.

23. Cf. Freud's words in the lecture on symbolism in the dream: 'The dreamer has at his disposal a symbolic means of expression of which he is unconscious while awake, and does not recognize when he sees. That is as remarkable as if you should make the discovery that your chambermaid understands Sanskrit, although you know she was born in a Bohemian village and never learned the language.'

24. Milton, *Paradise Lost*, III.

25. The researchers discussed in detail how Hélène Smith, a shop assistant in Geneva, had been able to gain knowledge of Sanskrit. Flournoy manages to trace possible signs in the literary forms of Indology, with which she may have come into fleeting contact through an acquaintance. But above all it is de Saussure who conducts

the linguistic review. As his starting point he uses the two words 'atiêyâ ganapatinâmâ', with which Hélène, on 3 March 1895, inaugurated the Hindu cycle about Princess Simandini and Prince Sivrouka. Saussure interprets this phrase as a Sanskrit-like hybrid of the French, 'Je vous bénis au nom de Ganapati' (I bless you in the name of Ganapati). In a crushingly ingenious – but not entirely convincing – reconstruction he leaves no clue unexamined and spares no mental effort. Saussure suggests thus: 1. *Je* is forced to transform. Did there appear in her memory an exotic word for *je*? No, none. So she then takes at random 'a' instead of *je*. (Perhaps this 'a' is inspired by the English 'I', pronounced 'aï', but it is not necessarily so.) 2. 'Vous bénis' or 'bénis vous', for if the word for *je* was suggested by the English, it may follow that the English word order, however involuntarily, had come to mark the words placed immediately afterwards. Consequently, for 'bénis vous' the words 'tiê yâ' are given. *Yâ* may have been taken from the English 'you' (modified by the most dominant vowel in Sanskrit). *Tiê*, 'bénis', has no known origin, as is the case with the Martian language. 3. 'Au nom de Ganapati', Ganapati's name, quite simply, without the previous mechanism's rewriting; it could have been taken from anywhere. There remains 'au nom de', expressed as 'nâmâ', reminiscent of the German *Name*, perhaps a resurrection of the Sanskrit word *nâmâ*, which she could have picked up somewhere; and finally the construction that, opposite to French word order, could have come on the coat-tails of the German *Name*, after the German turn of phrase *in Gottes Namen, in Ganapatis Namen*. In brief, a gibberish that assembles its components however it can, and half the time is invented, with the only rule being to prevent the audience from suspecting that it has derived from the French. (That is, a form of *Abwehr*, 'warding off'.)

As for Flournoy, he wanted to ascribe *atiêyâ* to 'achoo!', the onomatopoeic word for sneeze, connected with the desire for benediction: 'bless you'. See Flournoy, *op. cit.* And with this the case could be said to be closed, albeit barely adequately. For the sake of clarity I've illustrated Saussure's reasoning in the following diagram:

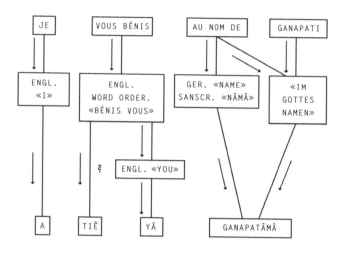

26. The nascent collaboration between early psychoanalysis and linguistics – so full of hope – was sealed genealogically with the marriage between Saussure's son and Théodore Flournoy's daughter.

27. In a footnote to his novel *Nadja,* André Breton confirms: 'Madame Sacco, *clairvoyante*, 3 rue des Usines, who has never been mistaken about me, assured me early this year that my mind was greatly occupied with

a "Hélène". Is this why, some time after this period, I was so greatly interested in everything concerning *Hélène Smith*? The conclusion is evidently on the order of that previously imposed upon me by the fusion in a dream of two extremely disparate images.' Hélène Smith's medial sensitivity seems to reverberate in the eponymous Nadja, who on one occasion exclaims: 'Hélène, c'est moi.' In surrealist mythology Smith is one of the great heroines, and like perennial favourites Freud, Marx, Sade, etc. she was honoured with her own playing card in the *Jeu de Marseille*, a deck of cards which the surrealists designed in 1941. There she represents 'knowledge' – placed between Hegel ('genius') and Paracelsus ('magic').

28. As it happens, in the French psychiatrist Pierre Janet's encompassing study of hysteria, *De l'angoisse à l'extase* (1928), he gives accounts of a series of detailed case studies. One of them regards a 28-year-old woman by the name of Nadia.

29. The author's observations here are presumably correct; great demands should be made for meticulous detective work, particularly in public legal affairs. Accordingly it can be of significance to follow each clue, for example to bring clarity to the snarls and passageways of the labyrinthine telephone network: 'District Chief Norberg has stated that the great number of reported errors with Kejne's home telephone were probably due to the rubber spiral attached to the microphone cable, per Pettersson's report, which was not approved by the telephone company, as well as to the loose screw in the cable distribution head... Faulty connections and disruptions during calls and attempted calls are considered normal phenomena caused by wear and tear, dirt and oxide accumulation in

the telephone exchange equipment, damp-damaged cables, greater or lesser problems with cables and defective telephones, and so on. Defective telephone exchange equipment could, for example, be caused by dust in the sockets, "friction" at various levels, burn damage from electrical currents, etc. Such defects could lead to faulty connections, "selector noise" ("fry" on the line) and similar.' From the files of the investigation by the Swedish Chancellor of Justice into allegations of illegal wiretapping in the Kejne Affair and certain allegations against members of the Kejne commission, etc., 1951.

30. Figure taken from the official government reports on the Kejne Affair, no. 21, 1951.

31. Cf. Jackson Pollock's painting, *Guardians of the Secret*, 1943.

32. That is to say, on one hand, preserve; on the other hand, invade it. Referring here to the Order of the Temple, established in the year 1118 in Jerusalem on the site of the ancient temple and tasked with protecting holy sites and Christian pilgrims. The Order's rules for this monk-like, military rank had been authored by Bernard de Clairvaux. The Knights Templar eventually came to possess incredible amounts of landed property and amassed vast treasures of gold and silver. Their immense riches in France were perhaps the key factor behind the conflict with the French King Philip the Fair. This wealth was also confiscated after a notorious trial that emerges as an eerie harbinger of the inquisitions of later times.

Several taboos were utilised in a way that may recall the great show trials and legal affairs of the 1930s and 1950s: sometimes purely ideological, sometimes sexual, sometimes both entwined. In a record from 9 November 1307 we can, for example, read the following about Hugues de Pairaud, a leader of the Knights Templar. When asked how he went about initiating new brothers, he responded under oath that after they promised not to reveal the Order's statutes or secrets, 'he led them to a secret place and caused himself to be kissed on the lower of the spine of the back, on the navel, and on the mouth, and afterwards caused a cross to be brought into the presence of whoever it was and told them that it was necessary, according to the statutes of the said Order, to deny the Crucified and the cross three times and to spit on the cross and the image of Jesus Christ crucified'. Georges Lizerand, ed., *Le Dossier de l'affaire des Templiers*. Vol. II, *Les Classiques de l'Histoire de France au Moyen âge*, 1923.

33. Minutes of the interrogation recorded in automatic writing by painter Ernst Josephson on the island of Bréhat at the onset of his schizophrenia. In these minutes the spirits (each in their own handwriting) confess, through Swedenborg's mediation, to a number of taboo violations relating to incest and homosexuality; in all, these minutes form a veritable dossier, a sheaf of pages measuring 18cm by 11.5cm, folded in half. On the first page, the name of the spirit is given along with a drawing of the spirit in profile, executed in seven strokes. Among these tormented spirits are the artist's relatives, kings, members of parliament, philosophers and the greats of world literature. Josephson imagines that he lives in the gatekeeper's lodge of the kingdom of heaven; in order to be granted entry by him the spirits must confess their most secret sins.

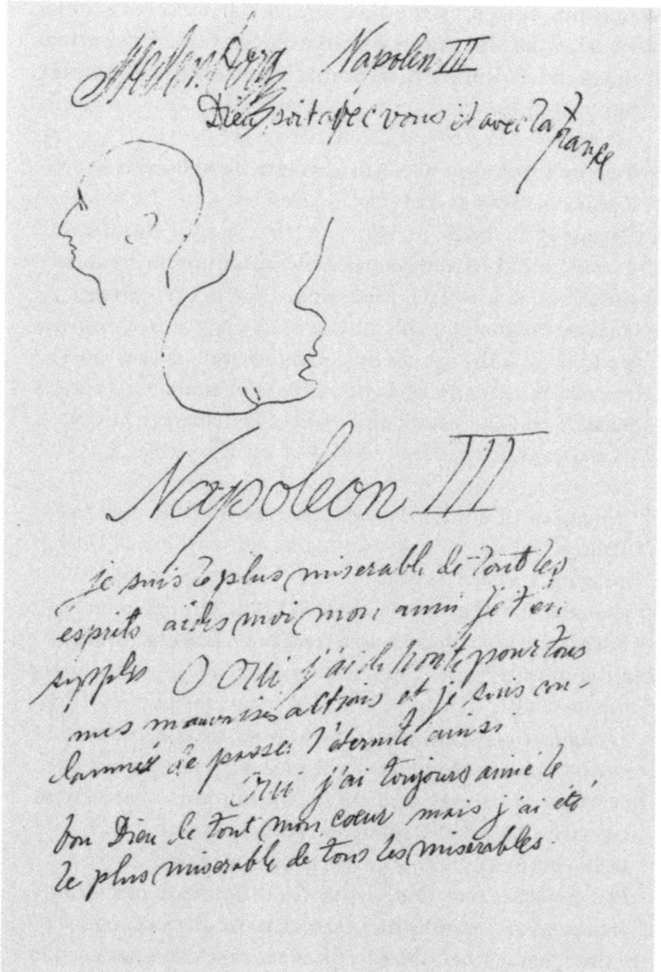

Ernst Josephson, *Napoléon III* (1888)

34. Despite the labyrinthine character of Moscow's major show trials, of which it is impossible to gain an overview, their centre is sometimes pointed out with astonishing clarity:

Vyshinsky: Bakayev, were you a member of the terrorist centre? Is that correct?
Bakayev: Yes, it is.
Vyshinsky: In 1932 did you receive instructions to organize the assassination of Comrade Stalin? Was that the case?
Bakayev: Yes.
Vyshinsky: You took a series of practical measures to carry out the act, that is, you organized several attempts to assassinate Comrade Stalin, which failed through no fault of your own?
Bakayev: Correct.
Vyshinsky: In addition, you took part in the assassination of Comrade Kirov?
Bakayev: Yes.
Vyshinsky: Furthermore, you travelled to Leningrad on assignment from the terrorist centre to monitor the preparations for the assassination?
Bakayev: Yes.
Vyshinsky: Upon returning from Leningrad, you reported that all was in order and that the preparations for the murder were proceeding successfully. During your visit did you meet with Kotolynov, Rumyantsev and others?
Bakayev: Yes.
Vyshinsky: Not only that, you met with Nikolayev, gave him instructions regarding the assassination and were convinced that he was a decisive person capable of carrying out said instructions?
Bakayev: Yes.

Confessions can in their willingness to oblige become so exemplary that they leave in their wake a feeling of emptiness and despair.

> *Vyshinsky*: How are the articles and statements you wrote in 1933, in which you gave the impression of being entirely dedicated to the Party, to be judged?
> As wilful deceit?
> *Kamenev*: No. It was worse than wilful deceit.
> *Vyshinsky*: A breach of faith?
> *Kamenev*: Worse.
> *Vyshinsky*: Worse than wilful deceit, worse than a breach of faith – can you find the word? Treason?
> *Kamenev*: You've found it.

> Cf. 'The Truth About the Trial Against the Terrorist Conspirators in Moscow', 1936.

35. Here see the very titling of the official documents, for example, 'United States of America v. Julius Rosenberg, Ethel Rosenberg, Anatoli A. Yakovlev, David Greenglass and Morton Sobell'.

36. The Grand Master of the Knights Templar, Jacques de Molay, confessed: 'Brother Humbert finally had an Arian cross with an image of the Crucified brought out and ordered me to deny this image of our Lord Jesus Christ. Reluctantly, I complied...' And Geoffroi de Charny confessed: 'After I had been received and dressed in a cloak, a cross with the effigy of our Lord Jesus Christ was brought in. Father Amaury said to me that I should not believe in the one here represented, for he was a false prophet, this was not God. Thrice he made me deny our Lord Jesus Christ.'

Almost all the Templars confessed under duress during their first interrogation that they had indulged in sodomy, that they had worshipped the idol Bahomet – a name heretically similar to 'Mahomet', the French name for Muhammad – and they had denied Christ.

Unlike the others accused, Molay and Charnay retracted their confessions before the papal tribunal sitting on 18 March 1314; on the express orders of the enraged king, they were burnt at the stake that very night.

At the stake, located in today's Place Dauphine, Jacques de Molay behaved in a dignified and stoic manner. King Philip the Fair himself witnessed the scene from a window of the nearby Palais de Justice. According to one witness, Molay cried out from the stake: 'God knows this is wrong. Woe shall soon befall those who have wrongly condemned us; God will avenge our death. I die with this conviction.'

Thirty-seven days later, the Pope died of a painful illness – he had condemned the Knights Templar in a special bull – and eight months later, Philip the Fair was thrown from his horse and killed; the same year the architect of the trial, Guillaume de Nogaret, also perished under mysterious circumstances. And, according to legend, the Templars' vengeance continued to be visited upon the king's offspring, vengeance that culminated in 1793 with the execution of King Louis XVI. The masses are said to have stormed the Bastille in tribute to Molay, who had been imprisoned there before his burning. And the legend only becomes more fantastical. It is said that during his imprisonment at the Bastille, Molay founded four masonic lodges, including one in Edinburgh and another in Stockholm. The task of these lodges was to guard the Templars' secrets and the memory of the iniquities and to become the executors of vengeance. They were sworn to eradicate all the kings of the Capetian line, weaken the pope's power, preach freedom for all people and to found a universal republic.

The heirs of the Knights Templar – the Jesuits sometimes included among them – are thereafter said to have been involved in various subversive and disruptive movements; legend has it they supported Cromwell, assassinated Henry IV and Gustav III, and lent their support to Swedenborg, Cagliostro and the Jacobins. This myth is formulated in the most fanciful way by Charles-Louis Cadet de Gassicourt, *Le tombeau de Jacques de Molay, ou le Secret des conspirateurs*, c. 1800; cf. J.M. Roberts, *The Mythology of the Secret Societies*, 1972; Auguste Viatte, *Les sources occultes du romantisme 1770–1820*, 1928.

37. Even Hwasser seems to accept such a possibility with these words: 'Whether great and true, if as yet undeveloped, ideas are in motion beneath the rich garb of fables, or whether their basic idea is in itself a deep and pervasive irony, remains to be seen.'

38. Places full of pain. 'Throughout his life, Masson painted "emblematic places"', Jean-Paul Clébert writes in his book about the French artist André Masson, *Mythologie d'André Masson* (1971). Masson served as a young private in World War I and was badly wounded at a place in Flanders that bore the name Chemin des Dames (Ladies' Way). Thereafter, he could never bring himself to stay in those parts. During much later travels through the region he was beset by chills, extremely sensitive to this bloodied geography that the very place names seem to have portended. There in the area of conflict lay, for example, Heurtebise (nigh on black, northerly wind); La Grotte du Dragon, where a massacre took place in 1917; and not far

from there the village of Soupir (sigh), Pontavert (bridge, warning) and Craonne, where he took up residence, which rouses associations with a skull. All coincidences that must be the work of chance, or, in Masson's words, 'what André Breton calls "objective chance"... Yes, I am a bit like Breton'.

39. The tunnel, the mouth of the Brunkeberg Tunnel. By chance Andrei Tarkovsky's choice of this peculiar and crowded urban space for the apocalyptic scenes in the movie *The Sacrifice* (1986) portend the scene of the murder.

40. Nadja reveals a new dimension in life and in the city. She talks about how she chose her name, 'because in Russian it's the beginning of the word hope, and because it's only the beginning'. Yet had Breton not chosen this name for it also conceals itself as an anagram in ArIADNe?

41. Coincidences or chance as the procuress of analogies. André Breton is of the opinion that 'objective chance' constitutes the very junction in what he has called the 'problem of all problems'. It is precisely objective chance that leads him to the life-changing encounter with the magnetic, fragile, eccentric Nadja. They meet in various places in the city, but their friendship ends when Nadja, like a roving spectre, disappears into the world of the mental institution. Their first, sudden encounter takes place on one of the dreary aimless afternoons during which Breton would roam around Paris: 'I had just crossed an intersection whose name I don't know, in front of a church. Suddenly, perhaps still ten feet away, I saw a young, poorly dressed woman walking toward me, she

had noticed me too, or perhaps had been watching me for several moments. She carried her head high, unlike everyone else on the pavement. And she looked so delicate she scarcely seemed to touch the ground as she walked. A faint smile may have been wandering across her face. She was curiously made up, as though beginning with her eyes, she had not had time to finish, though the rims of her eyes were dark for a blonde... I had never seen such eyes. Without a moment's hesitation, I spoke to this unknown woman, though I must admit that I expected the worst.'

42. Cf. Nadja's gait ('so delicate she scarcely seemed to touch the ground') with Gradiva's characteristically light steps.

43. 4 October 1926.

44. Indeed André Breton begins *Les vases communicants* (1932) with a motto from Wilhelm Jensen's novel *Gradiva*. And in 1937 he ran an art gallery of the same name on the rue de Seine. The entrance was made by Marcel Duchamp: visitors walked in and out of a doorway with a silhouette of the lovers from Breton's novel cut from glass.

45. A metamorphosis. In André Masson's painting *Gradiva* from 1939 – after Jensen's novel and Freud's essay – Gradiva is depicted in the moment of transformation between virginal, chaste marble and a living, physical body. It shows the very transition – or passage – between the classical object of art and the wild object of desire. In the background is a glimpse of the violent eruption of Vesuvius. Gradiva's torso is a piece of raw meat, her sex a toothed shell.

46. Cf. Marcel Duchamp's painting *Le Passage de la vierge à la mariée* (1912), with the transition, the metamorphosis from virgin to bride, noted in the painting's title.

47. Utterly superfluously the author conducts a systematic survey of the theme in Joyce, Kafka, Borges, Robbe-Grillet, et al.

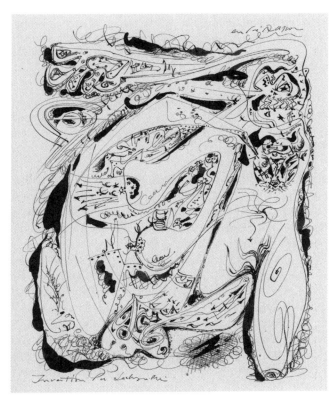

André Masson, *Invention of the Labyrinth* (1942)

48. It is correct to say that much of André Masson's artistic production circa 1940 revolves around the myth of the Cretan labyrinth. Indeed, it was Masson who, together with Bataille, christened the new surrealist journal *Minotaure* (the title *The Golden Age* had been in the running too). In *Invention of the Labyrinth*, Masson's ink drawing from 1942 (see above), the line seems to get lost in a turbulent, tangled jumble. Only after a while can we make out a few threads: a fragment of a coupling between Pasiphaë and the white bull; a chaos of limbs, sexuality, genitals and explosions. The work of art itself traces a journey through a labyrinth, in which the artist is Theseus and automatism his Ariadne's thread.

49. One example is Jackson Pollock's 1943 painting *Pasiphaë* (originally titled *Moby Dick*). Pollock painted it after seeing Masson's pastel of the same name in New York the same year.

50. Notably in Homer, Plutarch, Diodorus Siculus, Ovid, etc., King Minos of Crete receives from Poseidon the gift of a magnificent white bull, which is intended for sacrifice. Instead, Minos incorporates the creature into his herd and sacrifices a different bull. Poseidon then instils in Minos's wife Pasiphaë an irrepressible sexual desire for the white bull. Daedalus, the inventor, helps her by building a hollow, wooden cow decoy which Pasiphaë can enter, and there allow herself to be mounted by the bull.

As a result of this coupling, she births the Minotaur – half-human, half-monster. Minos wants to conceal and protect the Minotaur from the world and orders Daedalus to build a labyrinth, at the centre of which the Minotaur was to be placed. There the Minotaur fed on human sacrifices alone. Athens, too, had to contribute and was enjoined to send seven maidens and seven young men into the labyrinth every nine years. One day Theseus convinces his father, the King of Athens, to allow him to join this group of youths in order to destroy the Minotaur.

Upon arrival in Crete he meets Ariadne, daughter of Minos and Pasiphaë, and the two fall in love. Ariadne wants to help her beloved. She obtains a ball of thread from Daedalus that will enable Theseus to find his way out of the dark labyrinth. Theseus penetrates the labyrinth, kills the Minotaur and finds his way back out by following Ariadne's thread.

On Crete Minos rages and punishes Daedalus. He shuts him inside the labyrinth along with Daedalus's son Icarus. But Daedalus, as usual, finds a solution. He fashions large wings which he affixes to their bodies with wax. They escape the labyrinth by air, but Icarus, intoxicated by the joy of flight, soars higher and higher towards the sun. The heat of the sun melts the wax and Icarus falls into the sea.

Icarus's death does not, however, quench King Minos's thirst for vengeance. He searches for Daedalus throughout Magna Graecia, aided by a riddle: Who knows how to string a thread all the way through a spiral seashell and back again? At the home of King Cocalus (from the ancient Greek *koklos*, 'shell'), Minos finds a man who solves the riddle by making a small ant work its way through the winding shell with a thread. This man could be none other than Daedalus. However, Daedalus sensed the danger and, thanks to Cocalus's daughter, managed to scald Minos in the bath using an ingenious device that substituted boiling pitch for bath-water.

51. Note that despite the abundant references to the labyrinth in ancient literature, one cannot find a single author

who claims to have seen a labyrinth on Crete with their own eyes.

52. More precisely, an analogy or correspondence. 'It is not known, at the present day, what *correspondence* is... It was different for the ancients; for, to them, the science of correspondencies was the chief of all sciences.' Emanuel Swedenborg, *Heaven and Hell*, 1758.

53. Allow me to recall the etymology of the symbol. The Greek verb *symballein* roughly means 'to throw together', 'to unite'. In ancient Greece the noun derived from it, *symbolon*, characterized the sign of recognition created when a coin or bone fragment was broken in two to provide proof of identity between, for example, a messenger and the recipient. Each kept his own half, and when they met, each could verify the other's identity by checking that the two irregular edges along the breakage matched like two pieces of a puzzle. Figuratively speaking, the symbol therefore bears witness to an absent and otherwise invisible part. Cf. Thomas Aquinas's expression 'corporeal metaphors of spiritual things'.

54. 'Interestingly enough, neither Gold nor David Greenglass had originally remembered that the recognition signals they had shown each other had consisted of portions of a Jell-O box label. In his first statements to the FBI, David had recalled only that the signal was a cut or torn piece of card. And Gold, in his July 10 interrogation, had spoken of "two torn pieces of paper of an irregular shape, but which matched when put together". It was Ruth Greenglass, in her first signed statement of July 17, who identified the signal as the halves of a Jell-O box panel.' Joyce Milton and Ronald Radosh, *The Rosenberg*

File: A Search for the Truth, 1983.

55. 'Absens et presens' – an absent, heavenly and a present, earthly Jerusalem. The latter served as an incomplete image of the former. The value of visiting holy places has long been disputed. Whereas pilgrims like Chateaubriand do not for a moment evince doubt, Nerval doubts, and long before him, Church Father Gregory of Nyssa: 'When the Lord invites the blessed to their inheritance in the Kingdom of Heaven, He does not include a pilgrimage to Jerusalem among their good deeds. I knew the birth had taken place in Bethlehem long before I'd been there, in that very place. I knew of the Resurrection before I had seen the holy grave. Yes, do set off on a pilgrimage, but be it beyond the body and not from Cappadocia to Palestine!' However in the eschatological thinking that flourished around the year 1000, the wish to be in Jerusalem at the end of time grew ever stronger: it was then that the two Jerusalems were to meet.

56. Here returning to the concept of 'site' and 'nonsite'. The work of Robert Smithson occupies the field of tension between two poles: what he calls 'site' and 'nonsite'. He might begin his work by seeking out a site, a kind of magical boundary zone facing the void, typically an inaccessible, godforsaken, peripheral place: a desert, a quarry or an abandoned industrial wasteland. One such site would then become the starting point for a nonsite, which would take shape in the physical artwork, itself placed in a gallery. The nonsite was by its nature fragmentary, consisting of a pile of sand, rocks or earth that had been brought back from the original site and encased in geometrically shaped boxes, along with certain topographical documentation of their provenance, i.e. their

site. Smithson's site was materially absent and not easily accessible to the public; on the other hand, the public could partake in the corresponding nonsite physically present in the gallery. Between these two poles reigned a tension; one might even call it a longing. As Smithson put it: 'What you are really confronted with in a nonsite is the absence of the site... One is confronted with a very ponderous, weighty absence.' A nonsite is therefore a kind of signifier of and fabulation around an original and absent site. Robert Smithson's first nonsite was *A Nonsite, Pine Barrens, New Jersey* (1968). It consisted of containers of sand from a site in New Jersey, an old airfield with sandy runways. However, in his final nonsite, titled *Nonsite, Site Uncertain* (1968), any contact with an existing original site is tenuous and left open; the referent, for which 'nonsite' is the signifier, is dissolved. The artwork contains coal from somewhere in Ohio or Kentucky, but there is no information on the specific geographical location of this site – it seems to lose itself in time, in a distant geological carbon period. See Robert Hobbs, ed., *Robert Smithson: Sculpture*, 1981.

56a. Cf. utopia, from the ancient Greek ο τόπος, non-place.

57. 'Symbola' in Plato's *The Symposium*. In which it is told that once there was a human species of spherical androgynous beings that became so powerful they threatened the gods. Zeus came up with the idea of bisecting them into male and female halves. Plato uses the very term 'symbola' to designate these halves: 'Now, since the natural form of human beings had been cut in two, each half longed for the other.' That is to say, from then on, either half went in search of the half that was absent.

58. This phrase can be said to turn Gaston Bachelard's words into travesty: 'A comparison is often the beginning of a symbol, one which does not yet bear its full responsibility.' *La flamme d'une chandelle*, 1961.

59. An imitation of Novalis: 'Die Aufgabe in einem Buche das Universum zu finden.'

60. According to Colebrooke's estimation.

61. A similar question arises from the merely outlined, absent work, considered as a source for distinct, autonomous works. One could view Mallarmé's *The Book* and Marcel Duchamp's *The Green Box* from this perspective. The latter is a green cardboard box containing facsimiles of notes, documents and sketches, totalling 93 loose sheets, like Mallarmé's draft of *The Book*. The notes all relate to the 'great work' of Duchamp – who, like Mallarmé, was well aware of the alchemical resonances of this word – his large glass piece, *The Bride Stripped Bare by Her Bachelors, Even (The Large Glass)*. Duchamp's *The Green Box* was first published in 1934, although the notes date back to 1911–15, and so predate the completion of *The Large Glass*, which he began to execute in 1915 but only became 'definitively unfinished' in 1923. Despite the work in hand, the notes for *The Green Box* are extremely difficult to decipher, and so give rise to a growing number of interpretations. It would seem that the box lives a life of its own. Duchamp's notes are characterized by the same hermetic algebra, the same cryptic poetry that can be found in Mallarmé's sketches for *The Book*.

Marcel Duchamp, *The Green Box*

```
ALGEBRAIC COMPARISON
a/b
a being the exposition
b being the possibilities
```

the ratio a/b is in no way given by a number c, a/b = c but by the sign (/) which separates a and b; as soon as a and b are 'known' they become new units and lose their relative numerical value (or duration); the sign which separated them remains (sign of agreement or rather of…?…look for it!)

Stéphane Mallarmé, *The Book*, page 93

                                    480 the outer limit
                                         for a draft*

To obtain three times
   the evolution** 480 - identical to itself
 or deployed in the opposite direction

                                                960

through
160 x 3 - arranged so that 1st x 3, the 2nd x 3, etc.
all the way to the 10th
                = 48 (x 10 = 480 x 2 = 960)
                     or 96 x 10.

every séance or piece
is a game, a fragmen-   *fireworks
tary description, but   **veil, one of the aspects
as such sufficient.   in the book the yacht.
3 competitors, doubling

62. A relationship confirmed by Aragon's dedication of his novel *Le Paysan de Paris* to André Masson himself.

63. 'The metaphysics of place' – this expression is used by Louis Aragon in *Le Paysan de Paris*. In this novel the author explores the sacred places ('lieux sacrés') of the city of Paris. But these places, which he calls 'recreations of Ephesus', reside hidden in what is commonplace, and are unlike ancient places of religious worship in that they are not marked out by commemorative plaques or as tourist attractions. Instead in the heart of the noisy city, they lead discreet, as yet unrevealed existences, but are nonetheless a kind of node for modern mythologies. Aragon explores two of these places in *Le Paysan de Paris*: first, the great glassed-in passages of the Opéra (Galerie du Baromètre and Galerie du Thermomètre); then, in the latter part of the book, the forgotten Parc des Buttes-Chaumont of the Belleville district in the 19th arrondissement, a fair distance from the city centre. Both the park and the passages emerge as dreamy, anachronistic settings of a bygone era. The park is half in oblivion on the outskirts of Paris and the passages, which once heralded the apotheosis of the Second Empire and the arrival of a new era, were demolished shortly after the novel was published. Aragon takes the reader on a tour of these metaphysical places. He is conscientious and meticulous, like an ethnographer, a prolix guide who alternates between very precise information and imaginative associations.

In the tours of the passages, nothing escapes him. Everything is registered: restaurants, cafés (notably Café Certa, the Dadaists' café; 'It was while sitting here one afternoon, towards the end of 1919, that André Breton and I decided that this should henceforward become the meeting place for ourselves and our friends, a choice motivated partly by our loathing for Montparnasse and Montmartre, but partly also by the pleasure we derived from the equivocal atmosphere of the passages'), hairdressers, shops (their signs), menus, price lists, headlines exposing the controversy surrounding impending demolition, theatres and music halls. Yes, the author goes so far as to take us to one of the brothels in the passages, 'Mme Jehane, massage'. In Aragon's tour, the passages appear as dreamlike, seductive arrangements, fantastical aquariums bathed in muted blue-green light.

The Parc des Buttes-Chaumont was constructed around the same time as the arcades. Today a sign at the entrance to the park explains the site's motley history. For several centuries it was used for the gallows and as a repository for excrement from Paris's latrines. Then, little by little, the attractive geology of the site was exploited, with gypsum being mined in open quarries, which explains the dramatic irregularity of the terrain. It was under Napoleon III that an engineer by the name of Alphand was commissioned to transform this dour place into a park, a task into which he seems to have hurled himself body and soul, determined to realize his every passing fancy. The highest point of this romantic park is crowned by the Temple de la Sybille and linked to the other hills by two bridges: the 'suicide bridge' and a suspension bridge above an artificial lake. This is where, on an inky night, Aragon goes, accompanied by his two friends André Breton and Marcel Noll, following a whim of Breton's. The hills, caves, statues and monuments of the Buttes-Chaumont are described in detail. The three friends stroll through the park, conversing enthusiastically and indulging in the wildest speculations, like little boys on an adventure. In the warm night, the garden, with its unusual topography and amorous couples, acquires a special aura of euphoric mystery. According to Aragon, urban parks are remnants of man's longing for a lost paradise. Our love of a park's nature reveals an atavistic sensitivity to the mythical. The park conjures unconscious fantasies. It's the place where 'the city dwellers' wild dreams stir'; the 'décor of desires'.

64. A kind of broken optical instrument.

65. One could say that these labyrinthine arcades were zones for various forms of illusion-making. Here dioramas, mirrors, theatres and cinemas were all crowded, but these passages were also seductive in their commercial function, as forerunners of the modern department store. Goods were demonstrated to passers-by through illuminated shop windows displaying enticing scenographies. The wealth of society appeared as 'an immense accumulation of commodities', writes Marx in the first chapter of *Das Kapital*. Aragon describes the atmosphere of the arcades as suggestive, fickle and full of spectres; 'fantomatique', he says. This spectral world brings to mind the adjectives with which Marx characterizes the commodity: 'secret', 'enigmatic', 'supernatural', 'mysterious'. Commodities are 'fetishes', capable of 'somersaults' and 'metamorphoses' in their uninterrupted circulation between buyers and sellers.

66. This meeting place at Café Certa gave rise to the following birth certificate by Walter Benjamin: 'The father of Surrealism was Dada; its mother was an arcade. Dada, when the two first met, was already old.' Benjamin, *op. cit*.

67. In *Nadja* André Breton, more or less at random, passes by the following locations in Paris:

La place du Panthéon	La rue de la Chaussée-d'Antin
La place Maubert	La place Dauphine
Le boulevard de Bonne-Nouvelle	La rue Saint-Honoré
La porte Saint-Denis	La rue Saint-Georges
La rue Fontaine	La rue de Chéroy
(Breton's address)	(Nadja's address)
La rue de la Grange Batelière	Le quai Malaquais
Le passage de l'Opéra	La rue de Seine
Saint-Ouen	La rue de Varenne
La rue La Fayette	Le boulevard de Magenta
(where he encounters Nadja)	Le Palais-Royal
La rue du Faubourg-Poissonnière	Le boulevard Montmartre

68. Unbeknownst to him, he had nonetheless followed in the footsteps of other authors. Twenty years after *Nadja*, in the afterword to the book *Arcanum 17*, André Breton recalls: 'Just as, at the end of 1940, a long newspaper article inspired by the worst hatred of the time came to warn me that the route given in Paris to the "avengers of the Knights Templar" merged with the one I had unconsciously followed with Nadja, I had, guided by Monsieur Jean Richer's exegesis, no difficulty in convincing myself that here, on the purely symbolic level, I was walking with Nerval along the gilded path.' It is likely that Breton, at the time of writing, had recently become acquainted with the original cartographic survey of Nerval's imaginary esoteric world in Richer's study *Gérard de Nerval et les doctrines ésotériques*, 1947.

69. It is anonymous but is said to be by J. G. L. Kosegarten.

70. The surrealists circulate the city at random. They get to know and understand Paris by walking around. Their 'hermeneutic' flaneuring could be likened to an automatic drawing from Théodore Flournoy's *Esprits et médiums*

(1911), projected onto a map of Paris; they left similar traces.

71. Not Nadja. It's another woman: the 'scandalously beautiful' Jacqueline Lamba, whom André Breton met by chance at a Place Blanche café on 29 May 1934. That same evening, he followed her, the 'all-powerful commander', on a nocturnal stroll through Paris, to Les Halles, rue de Rivoli, the Île de la Cité, the Latin Quarter and Quai aux Fleurs. One of the most vibrant and frightening places they pass on their walk is the Tour Saint-Jacques on rue de Rivoli. It's as if Lamba had known, by some astonishing means, that this tower was one of the themes Breton had taken to heart, and that he, a few years earlier, had written these lines in the poem 'Vigilance':

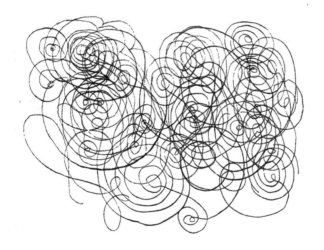

> À Paris la tour Saint-Jacques chancelante
> Pareille à un tournesol
>
> (The tower of Saint-Jacques, wavering like a sunflower [and with the double meaning of 'tournesol' in mind: 'litmus'])

One morning, a few days after this walk and while in a state of distraction, occupied by his morning toilette, a few phrases suddenly come to Breton's mind: words that turn out to be fragments of his own poem 'Tournesol', which he had almost forgotten because he'd never been particularly fond of it. 'Tournesol' is a 'poème automatique', from the surrealists' automatism period; Breton dates it back to 1923. And then, eleven years later, this poem calls to him. Breton digs it out, reads it and of a sudden it strikes him: it was a prophetic rendering of his nocturnal flaneuring with Lamba! Everything seems to fit, the state of mind, the places mentioned and the metaphors. Cf. A. Breton, *L'Amour fou*, 1937.

72. Ibid.

73. In the magazine *Minotaure* (no. 3–4, 1933), André Breton explores the passage to the surrealist paradise: automatism. He examines the relationship between surrealist automatism and that of mediums. Each can be characterized by a certain mechanics: the hand writes or draws as if of its own accord, and the owner of the hand can but marvel at the result. The main and crucial difference between them is, of course, that surrealism refuses to accept the existence of 'spirits'. The message, what is being dictated, emanates not from a spirit world on high, distinct from the medium, but from within: the human subconscious, the surrealists' holy land, or in Breton's

words, 'a common heritage'. Whereas spiritism *separates* the medium from the spirit, surrealism sees as its task to *unite* the human conscious with its unconscious. The article is richly illustrated with various automatic and medial drawings, such as *La maison de Mozart*, drawn by dramatist Victorien Sardou under Bernard Palissy's dictation, or Hélène Smith's drawings from *From India to the Planet Mars* and *From the Planet Mars to the Holy Land*. He also provides one of Nadja's drawings from the eponymous novel.

74. The handwriting in the posthumous *The Word of the Old Testament Explained*, which Emanuel Swedenborg 'wrote automatically', as well as in certain passages of *The Spiritual Diary* (1846), differs greatly from the regular handwriting in Swedenborg's other manuscripts; it is more angular, violent and illegible, and varies depending on which spirit is dictating the content. His own notes prove, beyond the shadow of a doubt, the hypothesis of automatic writing. In one passage, for example, he says: 'Nay I have written entire pages, and the spirits did not dictate the words, but absolutely guided my hand, so that it was they who were doing the writing.' Sometimes the automatism is associated with pure auditory dictation: 'These words... were said to me verbally and almost enunciated, and this by infants who were then with me and who also spake by my mouth and moreover directed my very hand.' Swedenborg's dictation experience calls to mind the definition of surrealism in the *First Manifesto of Surrealism* (1924) as 'psychic automatism in its pure state', i.e. 'dictated by thought, in the absence of any control exercised by reason'. Cf. Signe Toksvig, *Emanuel Swedenborg: Scientist and Mystic*, 1949.

75. Was said to be in possession of a yellowed book on the subject of Swedish tantrums.

76. The crossing to Île-de-Bréhat takes about ten minutes on the cutter that serves as a ferry. It was on this rocky island that Ernst Josephson descended into schizophrenia in 1888, the same year as Vincent van Gogh. Together with an artist friend named Allan Österlind, he had withdrawn to this place from the world, perhaps to lick his wounds after professional setbacks and trying conflicts within Konstnärsförbundet, the Swedish artists' association founded in opposition to the Royal Swedish Academy of Fine Arts. The progression of his illness is closely linked to automatism and his Swedenborgian studies. Josephson's automatic drawing arises following his contact with the French artist's wife, Madame Dupuis. This woman lived on Bréhat and was a devotee of what was emerging as one of her time's fashionable movements: spiritism. She treated it with the utmost earnestness, for the simple reason that she believed she could communicate daily with her son, who had drowned off the coast of Bréhat.

Madame Dupuis invited Josephson and Österlind to spiritist séances, the latter reporting: 'We took our seats around a table, which began to creak and rise from the ground and rush towards Josef. "Oh!" cried Madame Dupuis. "You, sir, are undoubtedly a great medium, you really should try your hand at it!" And so she taught us various ways of communicating with the spirits, in particular holding a pencil until the hand began to move of its own accord.'

The first drawings from Josephson's period of illness date back to these séances: simple line and figure drawings, signed by the spirits who guided his hand:

Michelangelo, Raphael and Rembrandt. 'Long into the night sat we around the table and followed J's hand in drawing', Österlind wrote in a letter.

Is there a common denominator between this spiritist automatism and the surrealist automatism of André Breton and Philippe Soupault, which they published in the book *The Magnetic Fields*? An authority such as Anna Balakian tries to tie up the threads and refers to Pierre Janet, a French professor of psychiatry who was practically the same age as Freud. André Breton, who had at first been a medical student, read Janet's books as part of his university education. During World War I, Breton served for a time in Saint-Dizier, where soldiers suffering from severe shock and psychosis were treated. Their obsessive thoughts, rambling speech and abnormal behaviour reinforced Breton's interest in psychiatry and in the discoveries of Freud and Janet. Balakian points out how a number of the key concepts of the surrealists can be traced back to Janet: 'magnetic fields' and 'automatism'. For Janet automatism is a state in which conscious control is relaxed. As an example, he suggests the situation in which we cannot remember how to spell a name; it has, so to speak, fallen out of our mind. We can't *think* our way to the correct spelling; however, in a state of distraction, we can suddenly find it again by writing in a relaxed manner: 'Allow the pen to run,' advises Janet, 'automatically, just as a medium queries their inner being.' Janet studied medial phenomena, but, like Théodore Flournoy, he maintained that these were not related to supernatural contact with the spirit world; on the contrary, their origins rested in the layers of the human subconscious and automatism was a means of making them accessible. Researchers other than Balakian – among them Breton himself – have chosen to downplay Janet's role and instead highlight

F. W. H. Myers, the British researcher who founded a psychological research institute devoted to various paranormal phenomena.

Whatever the case, it's clear that the surrealists had a predilection for the early pioneers of psychoanalysis, including Freud, Janet, Flournoy and Myers – with the exception of C. G. Jung, who, in their opinion, had betrayed the revolutionary character of psychoanalytic theory. The surrealists must have been seduced by the atmosphere of fantasy, magnetism, mediums and hysteria that surrounded the burgeoning psychoanalytic research. Thus, both Janet and Myers shared Freud's interest in hysteria. Janet describes the ecstasy of hysterical women in terms that would later be used by Breton, such as *amour fou* (mad love) or *convulsive*. For the surrealists early psychoanalytical studies revealed the poetic and aesthetic dimension of hysteria. It follows that Aragon and Breton devoted a double-page spread in *La Révolution surréaliste* (no. 11, 1928) to a tribute to hysteria on its fiftieth birthday: 'We surrealists insist on celebrating the fiftieth anniversary of hysteria, the greatest poetic discovery of the latter nineteenth century.' This tribute is illustrated with photographs from Dr Charcot's archives at La Salpêtrière: women animated by childlike, passionate gestures, erotic clairvoyants and fairies. Cf. Anna Balakian, *André Breton: Magus of Surrealism*, 1971; Sarane Alexandrian, *op. cit*.

77. The copyist.

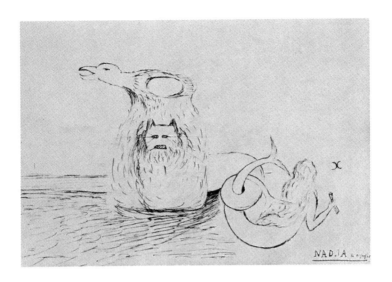

André Breton, *Un portrait symbolique d'elle et de moi...* from *Nadja* (1928)

III.

1. In this context the ephemeral labyrinthine traces made by the folds and creases of garments are close at hand. A considerable amount of older European painting has been devoted to the structure of such folds. In Rogier van der Weyden's painting *The Magdalen Reading*, dating from the mid-fifteenth century, the eye follows, as if hypnotized, the meandering folds of Magdalen's green dress. The costume, which is usually peripheral to literary motif, becomes central to the work. It creates space for a paradoxical element of free, abstract painting in the middle of the century's meticulous Flemish realism. Here we sense, smuggled into and camouflaged by a garment, a whisper of European mysticism – provided that one doesn't prefer, in the spirit of the Danish Marxist R. K. A. Broby-Johansen, to view the abundance of folds as a reflection of the expanding Flemish textile industry.

During a mescaline experiment, Aldous Huxley observed such a crumpled geography in Botticelli's *Judith*, as well as in his own plain, grey trousers. There he found a message about 'pure Being', Meister Eckhart's *Istigkeit*:

> My attention was arrested and I gazed in fascination, not at the pale neurotic heroine or her attendant, not at the victim's hairy head or the vernal landscape in the background, but at the purplish silk of Judith's pleated bodice and long wind-blown skirts.
>
> This was something I had seen before – seen that very morning, between the flowers and the furniture, when I looked down by chance, and went on passionately staring by choice, at my own crossed legs. Those folds in the trousers – what a labyrinth of endlessly significant complexity! And the texture of the grey flannel – how rich, how deeply,

mysteriously sumptuous! And here they were again, in Botticelli's picture...

Poring over Judith's skirts... I knew that Botticelli – and not Botticelli alone, but many others too – had looked at draperies with the same transfigured and transfiguring eyes as had been mine that morning. They had seen the *Istigkeit*, the Allness and Infinity of folded cloth and had done their best to render it in paint or stone. Necessarily, of course, without success. For the glory and the wonder of pure existence belong to another order, beyond the Power of even the highest art to express. But in Judith's skirt I could clearly see what, if I had been a painter of genius, I might have made of my old grey flannels. Not much, heaven knows, in comparison with the reality, but enough to delight generation after generation of beholders, enough to make them understand at least a little of the true significance of what, in our pathetic imbecility, we call 'mere things' and disregard in favour of television.
— Aldous Huxley, *The Doors of Perception*, 1954.

2. According to an old legend, Mary Magdalene, after the crucifixion, is said to have been led by a star to a mountain in Provence. There she went on to live in a grotto.

3. One is reminded of Mallarmé's reflections on the mysteries buried in the folds of pamphlets. Breaking the seal is both a compelling and painful violation, like the conquest of a young virgin or a holy walled city. Mallarmé writes in *Divagations*:

> Here, in the case at hand, is what I do: when it comes to booklets to read, according to common usage, I brandish my knife, like a poultry butcher.
>   The virgin folds of a new book, still, lend themselves to a

sacrifice whose blood stained the edges of ancient volumes red: they await the introduction of a weapon, or paper cutter, in order for possession to take place... However blind and haphazard, the strike is used up in the destruction of a frail inviolability. Sympathy would go to journalism, sheltered from this treatment: its influence is nevertheless unfortunate, imposing on the organism, complex, required by literature, the divine book, a certain monotony – it's always that same intolerable column that is distributed, made to the dimensions of the page, hundreds and hundreds of times.

4. Cf. the labyrinthine folds of Leonardo da Vinci's painting *The Virgin and Child with Saint Anne* (ca. 1503–19), a depiction of the Christ child, Mary and Mary's mother Anne.

In 1910 Sigmund Freud attempted to trace in detail the psychosexual evolution of Leonardo in his study 'Eine Kindheitserinnerung des Leonardo da Vinci'. He pored over piles of Leonardo's manuscripts on art, science and inventions, but could find only a single fragment on his private character. In a chapter on bird flight, Leonardo abruptly recalls that when he was an infant lying in his cradle, a vulture had come flying, landed next to him and thrust the plume of its tail into his mouth. This seemingly insignificant fragment is the starting point for Freud's research; it becomes the thread that Freud follows to uncover the most secret sides of Da Vinci and his oeuvre. And by the end of the study, his entire character seems to have been elucidated: Leonardo's latent homosexuality as well as his prodigious faculties for sublimation. The vulture is unmasked as a symbol of the mother because maternal attachment is one of the artist's major themes. The *Mona Lisa* represents both a gentle mother and a vampiric lover, *The Virgin and Child with Saint Anne* turns out to be a double portrait of maternity. Case closed.

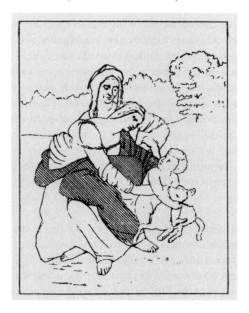

However, shortly after the publication of Freud's essay, his friend Oskar Pfister made a sensational discovery. If the mother, masked as a vulture, appears in Leonardo's only recovered childhood memory, or rather in his childhood fantasy, how is it that the vulture appears nowhere in his work? Well, it's precisely in the painting *The Virgin and Child with Saint Anne* that he finds the vulture, half-hidden in the folds of Mary's garments! The meandering of the folds must have been painted automatically; the brush must have been guided by the dictations of the unconscious. It was only afterwards, yes, only then that the distinct and surprising content of the folds was revealed. Pfister sketched out a diagram for all to see what he himself had seen: the vulture supine on the Virgin Mary's lap. The vulture's head, with its distinctive beak, rests along her back; one wing hangs over her right leg; and the cloth across her left arm constitutes the vulture's tail feathers –indeed angled towards the Christ Child's/ Leonardo's mouth. Mary's garment is metamorphosed, acquiring the character of a symbol. It refers to something absent and invisible, but not to pure Being, as in the folds of Botticelli's *Judith*, but rather to an unconscious, repressed and forgotten desire. Since then, a researcher has pointed out that the Italian *nibbio*, used in Leonardo's memory fragment, is not in fact the word for 'vulture', but for the bird we call a kite.

5. Sigmund Freud as writer or as man of science and tireless drainer of the Zuiderzee? As the eternally unhampered interpreter he is unsurpassed, whatever the veracity of his theory. A researcher such as Allan Megill finds *The Interpretation of Dreams* to be a wholly brilliant work, even if every single one of the book's conclusions has been proven wrong (*op. cit.*). Mircea Eliade too calls attention to Freud as a writer and myth-maker, rather than as a man of science. As he writes in his diary in December 1960: 'The interpretations proposed by Freud are more and more successful because they are among the myths accessible to modern man. The myth of the murdered father, among others, reconstituted and interpreted in *Totem and Taboo*. It would be impossible to ferret out a single example of slaying the father in primitive religions or mythologies. This *myth* was created by Freud. And what is more interesting: the intellectual elite accept it (is it because they understand it? Or because it is "true" for modern man?).' Or, in other words: perhaps Freud is

more poet than rabbi. Eliade, *Fragments d'un journal*, 1973.

6. Not how it happened.

7. 'Coming level with the Rue de Meaux we failed to notice the red dotted line which traces the border between the Quartier de La Villette and the Quartier du Combat. We had already passed the Bolivar Métro station where the Rue Bolivar is terminated by a spiral staircase, having started off among the rich pastures of new business and residential blocks. The Rue Secrétan then starts up, finally reaching the great Paving-stone depot not far from the Jacquard vocational school. Thus it is that, at the approaches to the park *in which nestles the town's collective unconscious*.' Aragon, *Le Paysan de Paris* (italics mine; in reference to the Parc des Buttes-Chaumont).

8. Humlegården as the 'town's collective unconscious'. Cf. here Ernst Josephson's 1888 medical file from the mental hospital in Uppsala. The painter had just been repatriated to Sweden from the island of Bréhat. 'Appears to have no hallucinations at present, but had before. (He claims to have seen smoke and vapours and sensed a foul smell rising from several parts of Humlegården in Stockholm.) His memory is generally good. Thinking apparatus lively, rash. False notions: he believes that all men of honour, among whom he counts himself, are being persecuted by a gang of Freemasons and Seraphim (Knights of the Royal Order of the Seraphim).'

9. Characterizing parks as 'the décor of desires' (Aragon) brings to mind the labyrinths of love that were in vogue in landscape architecture between 1550 and 1650. These labyrinths – resonant of ancient, magical, fertility rites

– gave allegorical shape to the convolutions of love. They were made of high trimmed hedges arranged in concentric circles, following a pattern that seems to have its origins in French church labyrinths. The hedges provided an ideal haven for the secret exchange of kisses and a hiding place for intimate encounters. At the centre of these labyrinths of love, a maypole was placed, as a fertility symbol and a reminder of the tree of life in paradise. See H. Kern, *op. cit.*

10. On the subject of parks as a starting point for labyrinthine urban wanderings, see report no. 21, 1951 in the Swedish Public Inquiry Commission Reports archive:

> Nilsson's statements, with the consent of the Prison Administration and at the request of District Commissioner Zetterqvist, led to the aforementioned being brought to Stockholm, where on 21 June 1950 he was taken around in order to identify the building in which the pastor lived. The transport went on for two hours and was led by Winberg, assisted by Paulsson. Before the transport began Nilsson was asked if he hadn't heard the name of the pastor in question and if he couldn't remember on which street the pastor lived. Nilsson responded thus: he could not remember the pastor having offered his name; regarding the street, he only knew that it 'lay in the southerly Söder neighbourhood'. The transport to the scene, which began at Humlegården, thereafter followed Nilsson's directions, and it transpired that, once south of Slussen in the Old Town, Nilsson was unable, despite painstaking examination, to locate the building inside which he had been. Finally Nilsson asserted that he was certain the pastor's home was located east of Götgatan, on a steeply sloping street that led to a crest and was lined with old, low wooden houses. The

pastor is said to have lived on the second floor of a stone building. Nilsson could only remember the shape of the staircase – a spiral – and that there was but one door on each landing.

'Investigation by the Swedish Chancellor of Justice into the Kejne Affair, etc.', 1951.

11. More precisely, the National Library of Sweden, built in Humlegården (Cf. Aragon's words, 'where the city dwellers' wild dreams stir'.)

12. The park as the city's wilderness, alluding to the enigmatic Berzelii Riots which took place in Stockholm in the summer of 1951. In the small hours of the night, Berzelii Park became a meeting place for people from the underworld: prostitutes of both sexes, pimps and other trouble-makers. Fights and disturbing displays of behaviour broke out with regularity, attracting crowds of curious night wanderers. The daily newspaper *Dagens Nyheter* reports on the violent night between 25th and 26th August: 'The crowd then retreated to Berzelii Park, which in a few moments crowded with people. Howls and whistles filled the air, and the atmosphere became ever more tense. Each policeman drew his weapons and, with great swift movements, drove the crowd out into the small streets adjacent to the park.'

13. Here, it is hardly necessary to underline the Hegelian influence.

14. Hagaparken, without a doubt. The Swedish spy Enbom lived in a cave in this park during the summer of 1951.

15. The State and the Media v. the Enbom Gang. Images of an overgrown child and fabulist daydreamer emerge from the descriptions of people who knew the man now incarcerated for life:

> To begin with, it is said of him that his clothes were never brushed, the collar of his overcoat covered with thick layers of dust and hair, and so on. His superiors would reprimand him for such things, and he was known to reply that he wasn't made to be a railwayman. Sometimes the rail traffic inspector had to order him to put on a clean shirt. 'And the very next day, he'd wear an immaculate white shirt, but only for one day.'
>
> Remarks of this kind about his outward appearance have been made by nearly all who knew him at the time and who provided testimonies. He is characterized as having a dirty and unkempt appearance even in uniform. He did not cut his hair. He had to be told to wash and take care of himself. His clothing was at times in tatters.

Excerpt from Gunnar Inghe and Gustav Jonsson's statements. Cf. Clarté, no. 1–2, 1953; Arne Trankell, op. cit.

16. '[T]o the utmost degree unkempt in his outward appearance.' Martin Lamm continues: 'Lidén, who had met him [Swedenborg] in London in 1769, says, "His clothing was soiled and even sordid; his face and hands appeared not to have been washed for several years". The Pastor Ferelius of the Swedish Legation tells us that Swedenborg never washed his face or hands and never brushed his clothes, "saying that neither dust nor filth stuck to him"'. Martin Lamm, *Swedenborg*, 1915.

17. According to C. G. Jung in *Wandlungen und Symbole*

der Libido (1911–12), an Eastern legend tells us that the Crusaders, in order to become invulnerable, smeared themselves with the pope's excrement.

18. Ibid. Jung writes: 'As is easily seen from the intimate connection of faeces and gold. Here the most worthless comes into the closest relation with the most valuable.' Alchemists were searching for their *prima materia* in excrement, one of the most cryptic substances out of which they hoped to see the mystical figure of the *filius philosophorum* emerge.

19. That is, not only among neurotics. A seemingly paradoxical identification between gold and waste matter seems to be widespread in the human imagination. In *Charakter und Analerotik* (1908), Freud references several analogous notions. He says they may stem from the fact that gold and ordure represent the most and least valuable things according to man; as the two poles in a pair of opposites, the association is easy to make. In certain archaic cultures that use shells as a form of payment, shells are referred to as the excrement of the sea. See also N. O. Brown, *op. cit.*

20. Freud's Hungarian colleague Sándor Ferenczi put forth that excrement is a child's first toy. In the child's pleasure-filled play, excrement will eventually be replaced by other, more cleanly substances, such as clay and mud – odourless variants of excrement. And clay is in turn replaced by cleaner, drier, adult-approved materials: sand in the sandbox, which manages to retain the same ersatz function in children's play. Nevertheless, children sometimes fall back into the messier stage by pouring water or even their own urine into the sand. Of the sand,

they make cakes; this can be interpreted as a remnant of the original coprophilic impulses.

At the next stage, small stones of different shapes and colours take the place of sand. Then follow glass or marbles, which are classified according to a hierarchy of value in the manner of primitive currency. And at the next level – the cleanest by all appearances – the marbles are replaced by money; we amass piles of money ('money does not stink'). A vestige of this link exists in language usage, as in the Swedish expression *besitta rikedom* ('to sit on one's money' or 'be in the possession of wealth', cf. the German *besitzen*). See Sándor Ferenczi, 'The ontogenesis of the interest in money', in *Zeitschrift für Psychoanalyse*, no. 2, 1914; Cf. also Norman O. Brown, *Life Against Death*, 1959.

21. Berch, for example, says: 'Whether he meant this seriously, or if it was just a mind game, remains unclear.'

22. He ordered tonnes of asphalt and glue to be poured, which ran down the slopes like lava. Cf. the description of Robert Smithson's 1971 work *Broken Circle/Spiral Hill* in Emmen, the Netherlands. *Broken Circle*: green water, white and yellow sand, four-metre-wide canal, four-metre-deep sand quarry; *Spiral Hill*: earth, black humus, white sand. Just as visitors were once taken aback by the clinical cleanliness of Mondrian's studio, the filth and disrepair of Smithson's studio did not fail to astonish.

23. The notes are in private hands.

24. A portion of the word has been torn away.

25. During his tour of the monuments of his childhood in

Passaic, New Jersey, Robert Smithson seems to glimpse his paradoxical paradise in a square sandbox, aka The Desert: 'The last monument was a sandbox or a model desert. Under the dead light of the Passaic afternoon the desert became a map of infinite disintegration and forgetfulness. This monument of minute particles blazed under a bleakly glowing sun, and suggested the sullen dissolution of entire continents, the drying up of oceans – no longer were there green forests and high mountains – all that existed were millions of grains of sand, a vast deposit of bones and stones pulverized into dust.'

26. The Jordanian plains around the cities of Sodom and Gomorrah were once as fertile as the Garden of Paradise, but were utterly ravaged by fire after the cities' destruction.

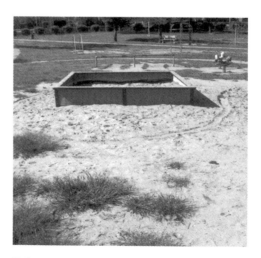

Robert Smithson, *The Desert* (1967)

27. Earthly paradise in the West. The collective imagination of American pioneers was strongly coloured by eschatological fantasies of earthly paradise. The first homesteaders' descriptions of the virginal land are impregnated with the myth of the Garden of Eden. It was taken as a sign, for example, that the state of Georgia was located on the same latitude as Palestine. Virginia was described as Canaan, 'a land of milk and honey', New England and Maryland as 'paradise on earth'. In the recurring prefix 'new' (New England, New Haven, New York) is an echo of the New Jerusalem. The pioneers drew comparisons between themselves and the people of Israel from the Old Testament: as the Jews had fled captivity in Egypt, they themselves had fled Europe, crossed a sea and reached the promised land. Yes, it was America that was designated as the ideal place for the Second Coming of Jesus Christ, according to the beliefs of seventeenth-century colonists (cf. Charles Sanford, *The Quest for Paradise*, 1961.) It was also in America that European utopian thinkers, such as Robert Owen in New Harmony and Étienne Cabet in Icaria, sought to realize their earthly paradises. These hopes and fantasies appear very much alive in the American unconscious. Nineteenth-century American painting bears witness to this imagining in its depiction of pristine, fertile expanses, awe-inspiring mountain ranges and bodies of water. Beyond the distant mountains in the West, the contours of Eden can be glimpsed. The same theme ran throughout twentieth-century regionalism, illustrated by the rural idylls of Grant Wood or Thomas Hart Benton, Jackson Pollock's teacher. Are the Land Art projects of the 1970s a paradoxical extension of the same mythology? In any case, we find in these artworks the same dizzying scale and the same quest for *sites*, sacred places of sorts. Land Art

has, however, shifted focus away from a land flowing with milk and honey to one of dry lake beds, salt lakes and infertile deserts – a land that may recall parts of biblical Palestine.

28. Expectantly and with devotion, Robert Smithson approached the shores of Utah's Great Salt Lake, the future setting for his *Spiral Jetty*: 'Slowly, we drew near to the lake, which resembled an impassive faint violet sheet held captive in a stony matrix, upon which the sun poured down its crushing light. An expanse of salt flats bordered the lake, and caught in its sediments were countless bits of wreckage. Old piers were left high and dry. The mere sight of the trapped fragments of junk and waste transported one into a world of modern prehistory. The products of a Devonian industry, the remains of a Silurian technology, all the machines of the Upper Carboniferous Period were lost in those expansive deposits of sand and mud.' Nancy Holt, ed., *The Writings of Robert Smithson*, 1979.

29. In his *Geographical Description of Palestine, or the Promised Land and Rocky Arabia* (1784; National Library of Sweden, rare collections), Anton Friedrich Büsching makes certain attempts to separate myths from travellers' observations, a laudable but delicate undertaking, as eyewitnesses were already hopelessly infected by the oldest story of all:

> This Lake is situated in that region, where in ancient times once lay the beautiful and fertile vale of Siddim, home to the five cities Sodom, Gomorrah, Admah, Zeboiim and Bela or Zoar, and which (like Egypt; Genesis 13:10) was traversed with innumerable canals and fosses... The valley

floor was full of bitumen, the pits of which are mentioned in Genesis 14:10. God's divine lightening bolt ignited these pits and all combustible material that was in this dell. The cities sank, and in place of the beautiful valley that Korte sought and where Dr Luther thought paradise to be is the lake we know today. Disputes are still being had over the remnants of the sunken cities present in this lake. The ruins are there, as credible witnesses can confirm, but whether they are from Sodom, as was claimed or believed, is another question...

On this island, in Troilo's account, a stone's throw from the shore of the lake, one can discern in the water the remnants of a ruined wall, perhaps fifteen fathoms long, which appears to be charred. As the ruin is not much submerged, he ventured there upon his mount and broke off a few stones as souvenirs; on contact with fire, they burnt like coal and gave off a vile odour and acrid smoke, likewise unburnt they had a stench.

Egmond van der Nijenburg, who was by this lake the day after Easter, perceived in the same place not only a pile of stones, but what were thought to be the ruins of a city uncovered by water; and he found on the beach large trees washed up by the waves, all of which appeared to be quite old.

30. Ibid.

31. With the exception of the artist's friend John Ruskin, the critics were acerbic; one coldly observed that William Holman Hunt's *The Scapegoat* (1854–56), for all its meticulous realism, was incapable of moving and interesting him more than last Sunday's leg of mutton. The suffering and emaciation of Hunt's scapegoat – intended as a representation of the goat that according to Jewish ritual

came to bear the sins of the people and was driven out into the desert – never quite succeeded in becoming truly transparent; that is to say, it did not succeed in expressing the corporeal metaphor of the spiritual thing, as Thomas Aquinas defined the symbol in his day.

And yet he had gone to incredible, uncompromising effort: Hunt had arrived at his destination, the Dead Sea, via Cairo. He rode on horseback to Jaffa, during the last and longest stage. He began his painting in October 1854 and worked on it from dawn to dusk throughout November, December, January, February, March, April... The region was rife with highwaymen and his servant continually threatened to abandon him. But on 10 May, at last he could note: 'The Scapegoat is finished.'

Hunt had carefully chosen the right place for his painting, a particularly barren plain, covered with salt deposits, located near the southernmost tip of the Dead Sea, a place alleged to be the site of ancient Sodom. He writes in his diary: 'But for a few acacia trees growing in the dry course of the storm-stream which we were following, there was no sign of vegetation anywhere... not a sign of humanity was before us... Every minute the mountains became more gorgeous and solemn... Afar all seemed of the brilliancy and preciousness of jewels, while near, it proved to be only salt and burnt lime, with decayed trees and broken branches brought down by the rivers feeding the lake. Skeletons of animals, which had perished for the most part in crossing the Jordan and the Jabbok, had been swept here and lay salt-covered, so that birds and beasts of prey left them untouched.' Cf. G.H. Fleming, *That Ne'er Shall Meet Again: Hunt, Millais and Rossetti*, 1971 and W.H. Hunt, *Pre-Raphaelitism and the Pre-Raphaelite Brotherhood*, 1905.

32. On the covering paper on the old back-board of the book, a brief catalogue of titles was found, which only became fully legible after the book itself was rebound in 1937. By all appearances it was a list of the books that William Holman Hunt took with him as a travel library or had acquired for his trip. Among them was *Narrative of a Journey Round the Dead Sea in the Bible Lands in 1850 and 1851* (1853) by Louis Félicien de Saulcy, a noble French archaeologist, philologist and explorer. Saulcy had an all-consuming interest in Palestine, particularly in its history, languages and geography. 'His workroom was a Jerusalem in miniature: antiquities, medallions, maps, engravings, plaster casts and photographs, all recalling and revolving around the Holy Land,' Wilhelm Froehner reports in a biography. The desiccated environs of the Dead Sea had not yet been the subject of any significant research. Saulcy claimed to have discovered the remnants of the ancient city of Sodom at the southern tip of the Dead Sea. The journey to this sea was arduous and known to be full of dangers; a number of explorers had lost their lives or been attacked and killed by the Bedouin tribes of the region. It was presumably Saulcy's evocative descriptions of the dramatic effects of light that strengthened the resolve of a deeply religious man like Hunt to paint *The Scapegoat* in situ. See Fernande Bassan, ed., *L.F. Caignart de Saulcy: Carnets de voyage en Orient, 1845–1869*, 1955.

33. 'In spite of it all, the camp provides a maximum sense of freedom.' This note was written from the remote Perm-36 camp by Russian dissident writer Andrei Sinyavsky. Later, as a refugee in Paris, he refused to sit at a desk; instead he wrote all his books sitting on the edge of his bed, a habit he retained from the difficult times in the camp.

34. In several letters.

35. 'The Orient is identified with commemorative *absence*. How else can we explain in the *Voyage*, a work of so original and individual a mind, the lazy use of large swatches of Lane, incorporated without a murmur by Nerval as *his* descriptions of the Orient?' writes Edward Said in *Orientalism*. In Gérard de Nerval's *Voyage en Orient*, the narrator is in search of a lost paradise, from Cairo to Beirut to Constantinople. He travels in circles, for the Holy Land does not allow focus to fall upon a single vanishing point; instead it dissolves into a vague absence. He avoids both Jerusalem and Nazareth. He believes himself to no longer be able to find the truth in these geographical locations – one of his travelling companions informs him that the angels have already transported the Virgin Mary's dwelling to Loreto, Italy and thus the detour to Nazareth is not worth the effort. The contemporary East he encounters on the journey is abandoned and in ruins. Nerval's voyage threatens to annihilate his Orient.

Instead, as we've seen, Nerval impregnates this modern landscape of disillusionment with mythologies and reveries drawn from his own reading, and for long spells this reading takes precedence over his real journey. Whole chapters of *Voyage en Orient* are simply compilations of works and travel accounts by other authors, such as Lane's *Modern Egyptians*, Creuzer's *La Symbolique et la mythologie des peuples anciens*, Herbelot's *Bibliothèque orientale*, Sacy's *Exposé de la religion des Druzes*, Abbé Terrasson's *Sethos* and many others. This book, thus, becomes a conjuration against the disappointments of his own journey, against his apprehensions that on his arrival the centre will turn to ash, or, as Nerval wrote in a letter to Théophile Gautier: 'I have already lost Kingdom upon Kingdom and province upon province and soon my fantasies will have no place of refuge; but I most regret having driven Egypt from my imagination, now that I have solemnly placed the country in my memory.'

The outline of a crumbling Sicilian labyrinth dating back to the Romans could be a figure and symbol of Nerval's route of travel. The dolphins outside the fortress wall suggest that the labyrinth comes from a city by the sea. The labyrinth is now housed in the archaeological museum of the city of Syracuse. The centre of the labyrinth itself has been left empty, a white square (cf. Aragon's words about Paris: 'the labyrinth without a Minotaur'). Over time, parts of the labyrinth have collapsed and its formerly cohesive structure has crumbled. The corridors and passages are no longer unconditionally subordinate to the centre, but instead compose a sort of liberated yet incoherent domain, a stage set for fanciful tales. Cf. Jean Richer, *op. cit.*; Edward W. Said, *Orientalism*, 1978.

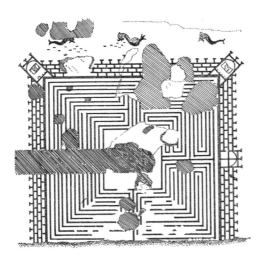

36. Clearly the imaginary representations engendered by the mere utterance of a place name can give rise to a world in itself detached from what those names designate. The young narrator of Marcel Proust's novel daydreams about the names of towns in Normandy and northern Italy: Balbec, Venice, Florence, Parma. 'But if their names thus permanently absorbed the image that I had formed of these towns, it was only by transforming that image, by subordinating its reappearance in me to their own special laws; and in consequence of this they made it more beautiful, but at the same time more different from anything that the towns of Normandy or Tuscany could in reality be, and, by increasing the arbitrary delights of my imagination, aggravated the disenchantment that was in store for me when I set out upon my travels. They magnified the idea that I formed of certain points on the earth's surface, making them more special, and in consequence more real.' Marcel Proust, *In Search of Lost Time. Swann's Way*, trans. C. K. Scott Moncrieff, 1922.

37. At the very turn of the century he rented a solitary cabin and set up camp by the disused Bibémus quarry. Paul Cézanne was then almost 60 years old. This retreat was a return to the place where, as a boy, he'd lived a free and happy life in the wilderness with his classmate Émile Zola. They had often swum in the great reservoir that Zola's father had constructed and which supplied the town of Aix with fresh water.

From Bibémus he had a view of his old subject, Mont Sainte-Victoire – looming there in the distance – and he reproduced it time and again. The quarry in the foreground lies bare, exposed to weather and wind and the merciless afternoon sun. Trees and bushes have begun to take root in the hollows of the ochre-coloured cliffs.

The area recalls the wild remnants of a strange, unkempt garden. A very particular disorder marks this place. John Rewald reports from a visit to the site: 'Yet it appears as though no plan presided over the exploitation of the quarry, where the stone has been extracted here and left untouched there. Between deep cavities and shallow furrows, solitary blocks remain standing.... It is a vast field of seemingly accidental forms, as if some prehistoric giant, constructing a fantastic playground, had piled up cubes and dug holes and then abandoned them without leaving a hint of his intricate plan.' The dramatic canvases of Bibémus confirm Dorival's impression that the artist had been 'seized by cosmic vertigo'. Everything, as in Erle Loran's diagram, is in uneasy motion and circulation. Cézanne said he wanted to paint 'the virginity of the world', its original state.

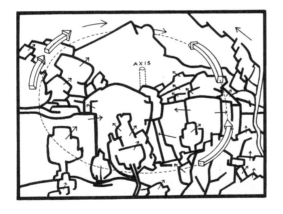

38. Probably in reference to the unfortunate Baron's observation in C. J. L. Almqvist's *Baron Julius K**:

Near Vättern

We continued our ascent of Mount Omberg and soon reached its most significant elevation close to Vättern. From here one has a vast and pleasant view across the water to the entire Västergötland coast, which stretches before the eye from north to south. The Vättern is among the deepest, most dangerous and turbulent of lakes, quick to roil and roll with terrible waves. Now it rested untroubled and gleamed with the clarity of a passion stilled.

Baron Julius was again walking at my side, and his spirit had returned to the melancholy in which we first encountered him, but which had taken on a more cheerful hue during our meal of wild strawberries.

Once at the point on the Omberg whence we were furnished with the immense view over water and land, we sat down in a circle so as to richly and at length enjoy this enchanting spectacle.

Each had his own observation.

The stranger said: 'Of all that I've seen on this earth, nothing so resembles Mount Carmel, albeit in miniature, as this, our Swedish Omberg.'

'Mount Carmel in Palestine!' Frans exclaimed. All eyes now fell upon our pale visitor.

'Has Monsieur le Baron visited Palestine?' I asked, rapt.

'I have climbed Mount Carmel', he replied with measure. 'Carmel, like this mountain, is neither very high nor peaked, but a broad, expansive plateau a few hundred feet above the mirror of the sea. Atop it one has a captivating view across the Mediterranean to the west, just as here the gaze looks out on our own little Mediterranean, Vättern. Were Tåkern at a greater distance from where we are, I'd compare it to Lake Tiberias or Genesareth. But one thing fails us: here there is no Lebanon in the background

to the north-east, unless we consider yon dark expanse of Kolmården or the Motala hills. Nor do we have Jerusalem on the plain below, nor the Cave of Elijah here upon our Swedish Carmel.'

'A journey to Palestine, to the Promised Land, in our time, in the nineteenth century, how unusual,' I remarked.

Image credits

6   August Westberg, *Kungliga Biblioteket, Humlegården Stockholm*, film printing, c. 21.6 x 30 cm, 1897. Tekniska Museet, Stockholm

11 Alice Roscher, *The Omphalos of Jerusalem*, drawing, taken from Wilhelm Heinrich Roscher, *Omphalos. Eine philologisch-archäologisch-volkskundliche Abhandlung über die Vorstellungen der Griechen und anderen Völker vom « Nabel der Erde »* [Omphalos: A Philological-Archaeological-Ethnographic Treatise on the Ideas of the Greeks and Other Peoples About the 'Centre of the Earth'] (Leipzig: Teubner, 1913), pl. IX

14 Robert Smithson, *Spiral Hill*, pencil and felt tip on paper, 40.6 x 30.5 cm, 1971. © Holt/Smithson Foundation, ADAGP, Paris

17 Michel Til, automatic drawing with quill, c. 1897, taken from Théodore Flournoy, *Esprits et médiums: Mélanges de métapsychique et de psychologie* [Spirits and Mediums: Blending Metaphysics and Psychology] (Geneva: Kündig, 1911), 104. © Gallica

20 Michael Wolgemut and Wilhelm Pleydenwurff, *Hierosolima*, print, 19 x 30 cm, 1493, taken from Hartmann Schedel, *Liber cronicarum*, 1493

22 Albrecht Dürer, 'Knot Design with Seven Hexagonal Stars', print, 28.5 x 22.5 cm, c. 1507. National Gallery of Art, Washington, Rosenwald Collection

23 Detail from Jackson Pollock, *Number 32*, oil painting on canvas, 269 x 457.5 cm, 1950. Kunstsammlung Nordrhein-Westphalen, Düsseldorf. Photograph by Walter Klein, Düsseldorf. © The Pollock-Krasner Foundation / Artists Rights Society (ARS), New York

26 Gottfried Eichler, 'Mundus', print, 23 x 15.7 cm, c. 1758; reproduced in Cesare Ripa, *Iconologia* (Augsburg: Johann Georg Hertel, 1758-60), pl. 6. Getty Research Institute, Los Angeles

29 Diagram taken from 'L'oubli des noms propres' [Forgetting Proper Names], in Sigmund Freud, *The Psychopathology of Everyday Life*, 1901, tr. Samuel Yankelevitch (Paris: Payot, 1922)

31 After Jean-Baptiste Lassus, taken from the labyrinth of Chartres Cathedral, 1859

34 Diagrams taken from Odilo Wolff, *Der Tempel von Jerusalem. Eine kunsthistorische Studie über seine Masse und Proportionen* [The Temple of Jerusalem: An Artistic and Historical Study of its Mass and Proportions] (Vienna: Verlag von Anton Schroll & Cie, 1913), 54 and 67

38 Frontmatter in *Cercle et Carré* [Circle and Square], drawing by Pierre Daura, 15 March 1930

40 Gérard de Nerval, *Les bords du Nil et ébauche d'un plan du Caire* [The Banks of the Nile and Sketch of a Plan of Cairo], ink and watercolour on paper, 15 x 9.5cm, taken from *Carnet de voyage en Orient* [Travelogue of a Journey in the Orient], 1843. Bibliothèque Nationale de France, Département des Archives et Manuscrits. © Gallica

46 Anonymous, 'Alle Weissheit ist bey Gott dem Herrn...', first chapter in *Siracide*, lithograph, 43.9 x 38 cm, 1654. Zentralbibliothek Zürich. Figure copied by Johann Kaspar Hiltensperger in a 1749 print

47 Jost Amman, 'Aus dem Geschlechterbuch der Familie Tucker' [From the Tucker family genealogy book], ink on parchment, 1589

55 Pilgrim clothes belonging to Stephan Praun: coats and hats made of felt, silk, wool and leather, bone and jet ornaments, shells; coconut tree wood and brass rosary; wood and iron stick with brass embellishments, 1571. Germanisches Nationalmuseum, Nürnberg

56 Paul Cézanne, *La Montagne Sainte-Victoire, vue de la carrière de Bibémus* [Sainte-Victoire Mountain, View from Bibémus], oil on canvas, 65.1 x 81.3 cm, 1895–99. Baltimore Museum of Art

57 Robert Smithson, *Spiral Jetty*, 1970. Photo by Gianfranco Gorgoni, film print, 16.2 x 24 cm, 1970. © Holt/Smithson Foundation & Dia Art Foundation, ADAGP, Paris

58 Attributed to Nikolai Suetin, photograph of the tomb of Kazimir Malevich in Nemchinovka, near Moscow, 1935, extract from *Kasimir Malewitsch zum 100 Geburtstag* (Cologne: Galerie Gmurzynska, 1978), 15

59 John Everett Millais, *John Ruskin*, oil on canvas, 78.7 x 68 cm, 1853–54. Ashmolean Museum, Oxford

60 Eugène Atget, 'House known as Nicolas Flamel's after restoration, or house of the Grand Pignon, 51 rue de Montmorency, 3rd arrondissement, Paris', print on albumen paper, 22.2 x 17.8 cm, c. 1900. Paris Musées / Musée Carnavalet – Histoire de Paris

61 The Virgil Master, miniature taken from the *Chroniques de France ou de Saint-Denis* [The Chronicles of France or of Saint-Denis], f. 48, parchment, 25 x 18 cm, c. 1380. Royal MS 20 C VII, British Library, London

62 Jackson Pollock, Ibid.

64 Paul-Marie-Léon Regnard, *Attitude Passionnelles: Érotisme* [Passionate Attitudes: Eroticism], photoengraving, 10.7 x 6.5 cm, 1878; taken from the *Iconographie photographique de la Salpêtrière (Service de M. Charcot)*, (Paris: Bureaux du progrès médical, 1878), pl. XIX et XXI. Getty Research Institute, Los Angeles

66 Francis Bedford, 'Upper Bethoron (Beit Ur al-Foqa and the Valley of Ajalon)', albumen print mounted on card, 23.1 x 29 cm, 1862. Royal Collection Trust

67 William Holman Hunt, *The Scapegoat*, oil on canvas, 86 x 140 cm, 1855. Lady Lever Art Gallery, Port Sunlight

68 André Masson, *Gradiva*, oil on canvas, 97 x 130 cm, 1939. Photo © Centre Pompidou, MNAM-CCI, RMN-Grand Palais. © ADAGP, Paris

69 Rogier van der Weyden, *The Magdalen Reading*, oil on wood, 62.2 x 54.4 cm, c. 1435. National Gallery, London

70 Blaise, 'Saint-Jacques-de-la-Boucherie', print, 15 x 11.6 cm, 1853; taken from Jacques-Antoine Dulaure, *Histoire physique, civile et morale de Paris depuis les premiers temps historiques, annotée et continuée jusqu'à nos jours par Camille Leynadier* [A Physical, Civil and Moral History of Paris from the Dawn of History, Annotated and Continued to the Present Day by Camille Leynadier] (Paris: Gabriel Roux éditeur, 1853), 17

74 Roger Henrard, *Vue aérienne de Paris avec l'île de la Cité et l'île Saint-Louis* [Aerial View of Paris With the Île de la Cité and the Île Saint-Louis] (detail), 1st, 4th and 6th arrondissements, silver gelatin print, 13.8 x19.8cm, 1952. © Paris Musées, Musée Carnavalet,

RMN-Grand Palais. All rights reserved

77   Diagram of the Golden Section, by the author

84   Diagram taken from Arthur Conan Doyle's novella 'The Adventure of the Naval Treaty', in *The Memoirs of Sherlock Holmes* (London: G. Newnes Ltd., 1894)

88   Diagram reproduced from 'Analysis of a Phobia in a Five-Year-Old Boy' ['Little Hans'], Sigmund Freud, 1909, in *Cinq psychanalyses* [Five Psychoanalyses], tr. Marie Bonaparte (Paris: Presses Universitaires de France, 1954)

92   Ernst Josephson, 'Napoléon III', drawing on paper, 17.7 x 11.5 cm, 1888. Nationalmuseum, Stockholm

99   André Masson, 'L'invention du labyrinthe' [The Invention of the Labyrinth], ink on paper, 58.7 x 46.4 cm, 1942. Museum of Modern Art, New York; gift of William S. Rubin. © ADAGP, Paris

111 Michel Til, Ibid.

117 André Breton, 'Un portrait symbolique d'elle et de moi...' [A Symbolic Portrait of Her and Me], photographic print of a drawing of Nadja, 1928. Reprinted by permission of Aube Ellouët-Breton et Atelier André Breton (www.andrebreton.fr). © ADAGP, Paris

122 Diagram by Oscar Pfister taken from 'L'oubli des noms propres' [Forgetting Proper Names], in Sigmund Freud, *The Psychopathology of Everyday Life*, 1901, tr. Samuel Yankelevitch (Paris: Payot, 1922)

130 Photograph taken from 'The Monuments of Passaic, New Jersey', *Artforum* VI, no. 4, December 1967. © Holt/Smithson Foundation, ADAGP, Paris, 2024

137 Copy of a mosaic from Taormina preserved in the Archaeological Museum of Syracuse, taken from Wiktor A. Daszewski, *Nea Paphos II*, 'La mosaïque de Thésée. Études sur les mosaïques avec représentations du labyrinthe, de Thésée et du Minotaure' [The Mosaic of Theseus: Studies on Mosaics Depicting the Labyrinth, Theseus and the Minotaur], Institute of Mediterranean and Oriental Cultures of the Polish Academy of Sciences (Warsaw: PWN, Éditions scientifiques de Pologne, 1977)

139 Diagram of the positioning of 'planes and volumes moving around an imaginary central axis' in 'La Montagne Sainte-Victoire, vue de la carrière de Bibémus' by Paul Cézanne, taken from Erle Loran, *Cézanne's Composition Analysis of His Form, with Diagrams and Photographs of His Motifs* (Berkeley/Los Angeles: University of California Press, 1943)

Works Cited

Louis Aragon, *Paris Peasant*, trans. Simon Watson Taylor (London: Pan Books, 1980)

Gaston Bachelard, *The Flame of a Candle*, trans. Joni Caldwell (Dallas: Dallas Institute Publications, 1988)

Gaston Bachelard, *The Poetics of Reverie: Childhood, Language, and the Cosmos*, trans. Daniel Russell (New York: Grossman, 1969)

Walter Benjamin, *The Arcades Project*, trans. Howard Eiland and Kevin MacLaughlin (Cambridge, MA: Belknap Press of Harvard University Press, 1999)

André Breton, *Nadja*, trans. Richard Howard (New York: Grove Press, 1960)

André Breton, *Manifestoes of Surrealism*, trans. Richard Seaver and Helen R. Lane (Ann Arbor: University of Michigan Press, 1969)

André Breton, 'The Fiftieth Anniversary of Hysteria', trans. Samuel Beckett, in *André Breton, What Is Surrealism?: Selected Writings*, ed. Franklin Rosemont (New York: Pathfinder Press, 1978)

André Breton, *Mad Love*, trans. Mary Ann Caws (Lincoln: University of Nebraska Press, 1987)

André Breton, 'Pont-Neuf', in *Free Rein*, trans. Michel Parmentier and Jacqueline d'Amboise (Lincoln: University of Nebraska Press, 1995)

André Breton, *Arcanum 17*, trans. Zack Rogow (Los Angeles: Green Integer, 2004)

Viscount de Chateaubriand, *Travels to Jerusalem and the Holy Land Through Egypt*, trans. Frederic Shoberl (London: Henry Colburn, 1835)

Jacques Derrida, 'Ellipsis', in *Writing and Difference*, trans. Alan Bass (Chicago: University of Chicago Press, 1978)

Mircea Eliade, *No Souvenirs: Journal, 1957–1969*, trans. Fred H. Johnson, Jr. (New York: Harper & Row, 1977)

Théodore Flournoy, *From India to the Planet Mars: A Study of a Case of Somnambulism with Glossolalia*, trans. Daniel B. Vermilye (New York: Harper & Brothers, 1900)

Sigmund Freud, *Psychopathology of Everyday Life*, trans. A. A. Brill (New York: Macmillan Company, 1914)

Sigmund Freud, 'The Dream: Symbolism in the Dream', in *A General Introduction to Psychoanalysis*, trans. G. Stanley Hall (New York: Horace Liveright, 1920)

Sigmund Freud, 'Delusions and Dreams in Jensen's *Gradiva*', in *The Standard Edition of the Complete Psychological Works of Sigmund Freud*, trans. James Strachey, vol. IX (1906-1908) (London: Hogarth Press, 1959)

Sigmund Freud, 'Creative Writers and Day-Dreaming', in *Collected Papers*, Vol. IV, trans. Joan Rivier, ed. Ernest Jones (New York: Basic Books, 1959)

Peter Handke, 'The Lesson of Mont Sainte-Victoire', in *Slow Homecoming*, trans. Ralph Manheim (New York: Farrar, Straus and Giroux, 1985)

Carl G. Jung, *Psychology of the Unconscious*, trans. Beatrice M. Hinkle (New York: Moffat, Yard, and Company, 1916)

Martin Lamm, *Emanuel Swedenborg: The Development of His Thought*, trans. Tomas Spiers and Anders Hallengren (West Chester, PA: Swedenborg Foundation, 2000)

André Lhote, *Treatise on Landscape Painting*, trans. W. J. Strachan (London: A. Zwemmer, 1950)

Kasimir Malevich, *The Non-Objective World*, trans. Howard Dearstyne (Chicago: Paul Theobald and Company, 1959)

Stéphane Mallarmé, 'The Book, Spiritual Instrument', trans. Michael Gibbs, in *New Wilderness Letter* (no. 11, December 1982)

Stéphane Mallarmé, *Divagations*, trans. Barbara Johnson (Cambridge, MA: Harvard University Press, 2007)

Gérard de Nerval, *Journey to the Orient*, trans. Norman Glass (New York: New York University Press, 1972)

Gérard de Nerval, *Journey to the Orient*, trans. Conrad Elphinstone (Antipodes Press: London, 2012)

Marcel Proust, *In Search of Lost Time*, trans. C. K. Scott Moncrieff (New Haven, CT: Yale University Press, 1987)

Marcel Proust, *On Reading Ruskin*, trans. Jean Autret, William Burford and Phillip J. Wolfe (New Haven, CT: Yale University Press, 1987)

Emanuel Swedenborg, *Heaven and Hell: Also the World of Spirits, or Intermediate State, from Things Heard and Seen*, rev. trans. (Boston: Massachusetts New-Church Union, 1889)

Emanuel Swedenborg, *The Word of the Old Testament Explained*, trans. Alfred Acton (Bryn Athyn, PA: Academy of the New Church, 1927)

All other translations by Saskia Vogel

Fitzcarraldo Editions
8-12 Creekside
London, SE8 3DX
Great Britain

Copyright © Peter Cornell, 1987
Translation copyright © Saskia Vogel, 2024
Originally published in Great Britain
by Fitzcarraldo Editions in 2024

The right of Peter Cornell to be identified as the
author of this work has been asserted in accordance with
Section 77 of the Copyright, Designs and Patents Act 1988.

ISBN 978-1-80427-106-3

Design by Ray O'Meara
Typeset in Fitzcarraldo
Printed and bound by TJ Books

All rights reserved. No part of this publication may be
reproduced, stored in a retrieval system or transmitted
in any form or by any means, electronic, mechanical,
photocopying, recording or otherwise, without prior
permission in writing from Fitzcarraldo Editions.

The cost of this translation was supported
by a subsidy from the Swedish Arts Council

fitzcarraldoeditions.com

Fitzcarraldo Editions